By Dia Calhoun

Firegold
Aria of the Sea
White Midnight
The Phoenix Dance

The Phoenix Dance

DIA CALHOUN

The Phoenix Dance

Farrar, Straus and Giroux / New York

I would like to thank Wesley Adams, Steven Chudney,
Kathryn O. Galbraith, and Dr. Mary Simonson for their help with this book.
Special thanks to my husband, Shawn Zink.

Copyright © 2005 by Dia Calhoun
All rights reserved
Distributed in Canada by Douglas & McIntyre Publishing Group
Printed in the United States of America
Designed by Jay Colvin
First edition, 2005
3 5 7 9 10 8 6 4 2

www.fsgkidsbooks.com

Library of Congress Cataloging-in-Publication Data
Calhoun, Dia.
   The Phoenix Dance / by Dia Calhoun.— 1st ed.
      p.   cm.
   Summary: Phoenix Dance battles an illness of her mind and emotions, realizes her
dream of becoming shoemaker to the Royal Household, and attempts to discover what
magic compels the twelve princesses of Windward to wear out their shoes each night.
Based on the fairy tale The twelve dancing princesses.
   ISBN-13: 978-0-374-35910-2
   ISBN-10: 0-374-35910-5
   [1. Fairy tales.   2. Mental illness—Fiction.   3. Self-perception—Fiction.
4. Emotions—Fiction.   5. Shoes—Fiction.   6. Princesses—Fiction.]   I. Title.

PZ7.C12747Ph 2005
[Fic]—dc22

2004056281

For all those who share Phoenix's struggle

There was once upon a time a King who had twelve daughters, each one more beautiful than the other. They all slept together in one chamber, in which their beds stood side by side, and every night when they were in them the King locked the door, and bolted it. But in the morning when he unlocked the door, he saw that their shoes were worn out with dancing, and no one could find out how that had come to pass.

—The Brothers Grimm, "The Twelve Dancing Princesses,"
translated by Margaret Hunt, 1884

The Phoenix Dance

1

Apprentice Wanted

A COLD WIND SLICED THROUGH Pearl Street as Phoenix Dance stood by the shoemaker's window staring at a sign wedged between a pair of black-and-white satin shoes. The sign said, in crudely written letters: *Apprentice wanted, inquire within.*

As Phoenix's cloak and her patched brown skirt blew around her, a twinge of excitement shot from her feet to the crown of her head. She could not believe her eyes. The sign had not been there yesterday, or the day before, or the day before that. Nearly every day for the past three months she had stood at this window dreaming of being the shoemaker's apprentice. Phoenix gazed at the exquisite shoes with their rhinestones and ribbons and rosettes, then touched the scrolling blue lettering painted on the window that said:

Percy Snailkips
Shoemaker to the Royal Household,
by Appointment to Her Majesty,
Queen Zandora
of the Royal House of Seaborne

Imagine making shoes for the queen! Phoenix smiled and clapped her hands. Why shouldn't she be Percy Snailkips's new apprentice?

A blur of movement rippled behind the glass; two people were coming out of the shop, probably to chase her away as usual. Before they could, Phoenix ran around the corner, down a side street, around another corner, and into the alley until she reached the rubbish can behind the shoemaker's shop. She took a deep breath and then lifted the lid off the can. The smell of rotting turnips assaulted her nose.

As Phoenix began picking through the garbage, bright treasures shone among the apple peels and soggy tea leaves—six brass beads, two crumpled peacock feathers, and a patch of glue-stained red velvet the size of her palm. Phoenix stuffed them into her cloak pocket. Her hands were cold, like the rest of her. On the island of Faranor, the capital of the archipelago kingdom of Windward, the late winter month of Zephyrus was always cold and wet, with chill winds blowing in from the islands in the Northern Reach. Phoenix had just spied a snippet of tapestry ribbon down deep when a door creaked.

"You!" A boy stuck his blond head out of the shoemaker's back door. Phoenix knew she should run, but she wanted that bit of ribbon.

"First you go pressing your hands and your snotty nose against the shop window," the boy said, "every day without fail. Saw you there a minute ago. Now I got to wash it off again. And here you are, snooping in the alley. How many times have I told you to keep clear of the shop? I'll set the guards on you, I swear I will."

"Go ahead," Phoenix said, moving a jar in the rubbish can.

"I'll see you rot in Five Towers Prison!" the boy exclaimed.

"Kloud's Thunder, what's all this racket?" And the shoemaker himself, Percy Snailkips, came to the door. "Why are you letting in all the cold wind, Alfred?" The shoemaker's brown leather apron bulged over his fat stomach. Beneath the apron, he wore a red shirt and brown pants. The wind ruffled the tufts of hair that fringed the top of his bald head. Phoenix gazed at him with awe. Had his sausage-like fingers really fashioned the delicate, fanciful shoes in the shop window?

"It's that snot-nosed beggar girl again," the boy said. "Picking through our trash."

"I'm no beggar." Phoenix reached for the tapestry ribbon. "I'm just looking for little pretties. You don't want them. You threw them out. I'm not hurting anything." She seized the ribbon, which was a good three inches long, and backed away. Now she could run.

"What do you want the scraps for?" The shoemaker scratched his head. "Making clothes for your dolly?"

"No!" Phoenix exclaimed. "I'm too old for dolls. I want them same as you, sir, for shoemaking."

He looked at her battered shoes with holes in the toes.

"For my aunts," she explained. "They're street dancers. Best you'll see in Faranor, too. And they need pretty doodads for their dancing slippers."

"I see." The shoemaker nodded. "So, Alfred, it seems we have a fellow shoemaker here. A person worthy of respect."

Alfred snorted.

"Wait a minute, girlie," the shoemaker said. "I have something for you." He went back inside the shop.

Phoenix hesitated. Should she run? The shoemaker might have gone to get a stick with which to beat her—she had been chased with sticks before. Then again, he might give her something pretty for her aunts' shoes. She decided that was worth the risk.

Alfred glared. "I don't know why he's being kind to rubbish." He wiped his scraggly blond hair away from his eyes, which were the color of toasted almonds. He was perhaps fourteen and as pudgy as a bun. Phoenix stared at him enviously. Lucky, lucky boy, she thought, to be Percy Snailkips's apprentice. He was allowed to touch the shining satins and ribbons, the deep velvets, the beads, laces, and brocades. He knew how to transform them into shoes in which people could walk, run, work, and dance.

"Is it true your master is looking for another apprentice?" Phoenix asked. "I saw the sign in the window."

"We don't take dirty beggar girls," he said.

Phoenix stuck out her tongue at him.

The shoemaker came back and held out a muslin bundle.

"Here are some more scraps," he said. "And two of my wife's muffins for good measure."

Phoenix drew herself up. She knew she looked like a scrap herself, as thin as the orange-striped alley cat slinking along the wall.

"I'm no beggar, sir," she said. "I wasn't looking for food."

"I know, I know," he said. "Just think of it as a present from one shoemaker to another." He grinned as she took the bundle. "Making shoes makes appetite. Now get along with you. And next time you want scraps, come knocking on the back door here. I'll keep the odds and ends for you."

Alfred scowled.

Phoenix almost asked the shoemaker about the apprenticeship, but the sign had said inquire within, and she was not within. She was outside, in the alley. She feared that would put her at a disadvantage. Besides, the shoemaker had already gone back inside the shop, and Alfred, with a parting sneer, was shutting the door. So, clutching the bundle, Phoenix ran down the alley. She crossed Admiral Square, then turned right onto Anemone Street, which led down to Harbor Road, where the merchants kept their stalls and stores, and vendors hawked their wares.

"Brickly-brick sweetie sticks!" called a woman pushing a cart loaded with chocolates, creams, toffees, nougats, fizzle suckers, and almond-coated queen's delights. Phoenix dodged around her.

"Fresh sea trotters! Fat sea trotters! Finest sea trotters you'll ever see!" shouted a man as he tossed a fish high into the air. It flashed and spun, and he caught it—*slap, slap*—in his arms. Phoenix laughed. How she loved the market!

All the shouting turned into a blur of sound:

"Fine carpets from the East!"

"See the jugglers!"

"Buy your bobbin lace here!"

"Apprentice wanted!" Phoenix shouted. "Inquire within!"

"Bowls from Boularry!"

"Silver from Silanon!"

Because Faranor was the capital of Windward, almost everything made in the kingdom eventually found its way to the busy shops and stalls on Harbor Road. An aviary sold exotic birds and stuffed wildcats from the Southern Reach. A magic shop sold charms, potions, crystals, and wizards' robes embroidered with moons and stars. Phoenix lingered by the window of a shop that sold silk from the Eastern Reach. She longed to have a dress that reached to her ankles instead of this old tight one that fell only to the bottoms of her calves. That pale green silk hanging from its bolt would look fine with her reddish brown hair and brown eyes.

Phoenix tore herself from the window and pushed her way through the crowd until she came to the Sea Dragon

Fountain in Sea Dragon Courtyard. The bronze sea dragon arched its neck and stretched its wings, rearing up amid the spurting jets of water as though it had just risen from the dark depths and was about to leap from the swirling pool into the sky. Flames, frozen in bronze, shot from its mouth. The sea dragon seemed almost real, as though a wizard had cast a spell upon it in the moment just before its fiery flight. Phoenix's aunts' troupe of street dancers, the Seven Sea Stars, often performed in front of the fountain, but to her disappointment, they were not there now.

Phoenix was aching to tell someone about the sign in the shoemaker's window. She looked for her best friend, Rora— short for Aurora—who often strode about the courtyard passing out pamphlets for the Archipelago Party, or making speeches against the monarchy and in favor of more representation in Parliament by the people. However, Rora was not there either.

"Where is everyone?" Phoenix muttered. "I have news, news, news!"

After darting in and out of the crowd for three more blocks, Phoenix turned onto a narrow street called Black Diamond Lane. Six houses down was her house, squeezed like a crooked tooth between two other houses. Red paint peeled off the front as though the house were suffering from a terrible sunburn. She climbed the rickety stairs to the top floor and reached the three shabby rooms where she lived with her aunts.

"Hello, hello!" Phoenix called, bursting in the orange-painted door. "I have news and treasure!" The parlor, painted a bright purple with marigold trim, made up in brightness what it lacked in elegance. Her aunts firmly believed in color, as they told the many artists, musicians, and poets who visited them.

"Treasure!" cried Aunt Twisle from the blue sofa. A rip along the back had been mended with bright green yarn and tassels on each end. Aunt Twisle put down the jester's costume she was sewing. "You're our treasure. Mulgaussy! Liona! Our Phoenix is home." Aunt Twisle's long hair fell as golden and straight as a sunbeam. She wore a red dress with a ruffled red skirt; Phoenix recognized it as one of the costumes from the ballet *The Dark Wizard's Revenge*. In one corner of the room, a stand heaped with costumes, hats, and wigs looked as though it might topple over at any moment. "We have news for you, too," Aunt Twisle added.

"Wait for me, sister! Don't tell her yet," Aunt Mulgaussy said as she hurried out from the bedchamber with a pile of knitting in her arms. Wispy and thin, she had skin that looked like cream poured on white satin. Because she was the most beautiful of the three aunts and the best dancer, she always danced the maidens in distress.

Aunt Liona strode in from the kitchen, beating yellow batter in a mixing bowl clutched to her waist. She was counting, "Ninety-eight, ninety-nine, one hundred—there!" She stopped beating. "That's done. Four cups of sugar. A dozen eggs. One hundred strokes. Whew." Two tortoiseshell combs held her curly black hair. The aunts were still young, in their early thirties. They had taken Phoenix in after her parents, Chalsawn and Aviel Dance, died of redwater fever when she was five.

"Wait to tell me what?" Phoenix asked, untying the muslin bundle the shoemaker had given her. "Look, corn muffins. Yum. What else did that shoemaker put in, what else, what else!"

"What shoemaker?" Aunt Twisle asked as the aunts leaned closer to see.

Phoenix gasped. There were four scraps of velvet—red, gold, white, and green. There were two blue silk rosettes with just a little black dye staining them. She could hide the stain with the crystal beads—only slightly cracked. Best of all, there were two mismatched brass buckles, only a little scuffed and dented. After she wrapped them with the velvet, the dents would not show.

"Oh, how beautiful, beautiful!" Phoenix cried. "I'll make dancing shoes pretty enough for a princess! And you, my lovely, lovely aunts, shall wear them. Just wait and see! I'll make shoes as fine as those in the shoemaker's window!" She took a scrap of velvet in each hand and began dancing around the room.

"She's getting wound up," Aunt Liona warned.

"*Getting* wound up?" asked Aunt Twisle. "She *is* wound up."

"She'll go off in one of her moods," Aunt Mulgaussy said. "Be glittery and flighty for days, bless her. And then she'll slip into the melancholy of the Nethersea."

"Don't worry, worry, worry!" Phoenix laughed at them and kept dancing. "Such treasures today! I'll make dazzling shoes for darling Aunt Mulgaussy. She'll be the prettiest dancer in Faranor! No, in all of Windward!"

"Calm down, Phoenix!" Aunt Twisle said.

"It's wonderful!" Phoenix sang. "A wonderful day! A shining treasure day! A sign in the window day! A bead and velvet and blue rosette day! Inquire within, inquire within!" She danced around the room until Aunt Twisle, always the sternest, grabbed her arm and pulled her down on the sofa.

"Listen, Phoenix," she said. "We have good news for you. Don't you want to hear it?"

"All right, all right. Yes, of course, right away. Tell me now. I can't believe the shoemaker was so kind to me. He said to come back whenever—"

"Phoenix!" Aunt Liona rapped the wooden spoon against the mixing bowl. "Listen. This is important. It's about your future."

"My future?" Phoenix asked. "About that—"

"You finished your standard schooling two months ago," Aunt Twisle interrupted. "I wish so much that you could go on to higher schooling, but you know that's beyond our means. So we must find a suitable occupation for you."

"You've just turned fourteen, the age to be apprenticed," Aunt Liona added.

"Exactly!" Phoenix cried. "That's my news! The shoemaker had a sign in his window today—apprentice wanted, inquire within. He's looking for an apprentice. I want to be his apprentice. I want to learn to make the most beautiful shoes in the kingdom!"

The room was silent.

"My darling, talented niece, apprentice to a shoemaker?" Aunt Mulgaussy asked. "Absolutely not."

"When sharks turn into lambs," said Aunt Liona.

"Never," said Aunt Twisle.

2

The Great-granddaughter of Seagraine Dance

BUT WHY CAN'T I APPRENTICE WITH the shoemaker?" Phoenix, who was still sitting on the blue sofa beside Aunt Twisle, threw down the velvet scraps she had been holding. They landed over the corn muffins on the low table in front of the sofa. "Why not?" she demanded.

Aunt Mulgaussy perched on the armrest of the over-stuffed chintz chair beside the table. In her white dress, she looked like a large bit of lint stuck to the chair. Her knitting, a long scarf of every color of the rainbow, spilled down the front of her dress and puddled at her feet.

"You know very well why not, dear," she said, picking up her knitting needles. "Because you are the great-granddaughter of Seagraine Dance, the former Duchess of the Islands of Trebonness. And the great-granddaughter of

Seagraine Dance does not make things for people to stick their dirty feet into."

Phoenix sighed. "Not that again." No one would ever guess from the way they lived that she and her aunts were descended from a duchess. Seagraine Dance, long dead, had gambled away the three islands of Trebonness in the Western Reach when Aunt Twisle was eight, Aunt Liona was seven, and Aunt Mulgaussy was five. Although the aunts were poor now, they never forgot they were descended from nobility. Phoenix considered it a burden. All it meant to her was that she had to sit up straighter than other girls, curtsy more gracefully, know how to use many different kinds of knives, forks, and spoons—even though she did not always have enough food to eat with them—and often could not do what she wanted to do.

"Besides," Aunt Twisle said, "we've just arranged an apprenticeship for you. That's what we've been trying to tell you. But you don't listen, do you?"

"We thought something in the arts would be dignified." Aunt Mulgaussy pulled more yellow yarn off the ball. "Even nobles sometimes become painters and musicians."

"Think of it!" Aunt Liona said. "Phoenix Dance, painter extraordinaire!" She grabbed the wooden spoon in the mixing bowl against her waist and flourished it like a brush. "I can see you now in a black beret with a brush in your hand and a dab of paint on your nose!"

"But the painters' apprentice fees were too high," Aunt Twisle said.

"So we thought of apprenticing you to the great actress Marina Selene," said Aunt Mulgaussy. "There's no brighter star in Faranor. How that woman can act! I weep just to see her walk onstage. But she, well, we couldn't afford her apprentice fee either, dear. If only we were still in Trebonness . . ." She sighed.

"If only we were still in Trebonness" was a common refrain whenever anything went wrong. The aunts dreamed of someday having the property restored to them. So did Phoenix, but only because, if they lived in Trebonness, she would have shoes without holes, dresses that were long enough, and always enough to eat.

"Next we talked to Ebbon Lloyd," Aunt Twisle said, "the actor. He's not so famous, of course, but he's a solid craftsman and—"

"And he's agreed to take you!" finished Aunt Liona. "Isn't that spectacular? Just spectacular? I'm making a pound cake to celebrate. A dozen eggs. What extravagance! Is this how the rich feel? Throwing eggs to the wind?"

"Me?" Phoenix asked. "Apprentice to an actor? Are you mad? I can't act. I can't sing. I can't dance. Or do any of those things that you three do. Graceful, swooping, dancing things."

"Nonsense," said Aunt Twisle. "Your mother was a dancer."

"And your father was an actor," added Aunt Mulgaussy. "Bless him."

"It must be in your blood somewhere," said Aunt Liona. "Just aching to get out. If you'd only try, Phoenix."

"No!" Phoenix exclaimed. "I don't want to be an actress. Nothing on a stage. I don't want a job like yours where I must drift from place to place. Actors have to travel. I want something solid. In a shop. Out of the rain. I want to work with my hands. I want to be a shoemaker!"

"But why something so . . . terribly common?" asked Aunt Twisle. "We've raised you with artists and musicians and dancers, with poets and philosophers. I know we're poor. I know we live crowded in these three little rooms and don't always have enough to eat. But we've fed you with ideas and art. Filled your mind with beauty and—"

"Not just any shoemaker," Phoenix interrupted, hurt by the bewildered disappointment on their faces. "I want to apprentice with Percy Snailkips."

"Snailkips?" said Aunt Mulgaussy faintly, reaching over to the costume rack. She plucked a straw hat and fanned herself with it, the blue ribbons waving back and forth. "Snail . . . kips? I'm sure there are no Snailkipses in Trebonness."

"He's the shoemaker to the queen herself," Phoenix said. "To the entire Royal Household. I'm sure they all have clean feet, Aunt Mulgaussy. Don't the nobles take baths every day? You should see the shoes in his window. They're works of art, they are! Like little sculptures. Something fine, all right. And today he put a sign up in his window advertising for an apprentice. He's the one who gave me these lovely scraps. I was digging in his garbage when—"

"Digging in his garbage!" all three aunts exclaimed.

"Well, where do you think I find the scraps to decorate your shoes? I visit all the rubbish cans behind all the shoe shops. You like the shoes I decorate for you, don't you?"

"Of course," said Aunt Liona. "But—garbage! That's abominable!"

"We don't want you digging in rubbish cans anymore," said Aunt Twisle.

"Absolutely not." Aunt Mulgaussy dropped the straw hat on the chair and speared it with one of her long needles. "It's not fitting—"

"I know," Phoenix interrupted. "It's not fitting for the great-granddaughter of Seagraine Dance. But I won't give up decorating shoes. I won't. Oh, please, don't ask me to. Oh, please, dear aunts, oh, please go talk to Percy Snailkips. You know I'm no good at acting or dancing. Please let me be a shoemaker. I'll make you the most beautiful dancing shoes in the kingdom!"

"Percy Snailkips," Aunt Twisle said, drumming her fingers on the table. "I've seen his shoes. Phoenix is right. Some are quite exquisite. They are little works of art. I've heard others speak well of him—though he is a staunch member of the Royalist Party."

"You forget, Twisle, I, too, am a staunch member of the

Royalist Party," said Aunt Mulgaussy. "That's a mark in the shoemaker's favor, in my mind."

There was a silence, broken only by the clicking of Aunt Mulgaussy's knitting needles. Aunt Twisle and Aunt Liona were loyal members of the Archipelago Party, and had opposite ideas from those in the Royalist Party. The three women frequently launched into long-winded political arguments, and Phoenix feared they were about to do so now.

"Percy Snailkips won't charge as large an apprentice fee as Ebbon Lloyd," she said quickly, to distract them. "Where are you going to get the money anyway?"

All three aunts looked at the curio cabinet on the far wall, where a ray of sun beaming through the window shone on the curving glass doors. Aunt Mulgaussy's sailor husband, Horace, had given her the cabinet on their wedding day. Each time he returned from a voyage he brought an exotic item for the shelves—including the skulls of a lemur and parrot; an ebony whistle; a pair of maracas made, Horace claimed, of human skin; a jade pendant; a series of exquisite nesting lacquered boxes; and several jars carved out of ivory. He had never returned from his last voyage, five years ago now, and his ship was considered lost at sea. Whenever Phoenix's aunts grew truly pinched for money, one of the curiosities disappeared.

"Not the nesting boxes!" Phoenix cried.

"You're not to worry about that, darling," Aunt Mulgaussy said. "Your uncle Horace would certainly approve. There now, today's row is finished. May he rest peacefully in the Sea Maid's arms." Every day Aunt Mulgaussy knitted one row onto her "Horace Scarf," as she called it, in memory of her husband. The scarf was now fifteen feet long.

"Maybe we should be practical, sisters," Aunt Liona said. "Why force Phoenix into an apprenticeship where she won't be happy? It's her life. Kloud's Bounty, she's old enough to know what she wants. Since this Percy Snailkips is Shoemaker to the Royal Household, he must be very respectable and we might at least consider an apprenticeship. Old Seagraine will never know."

"I'd be making shoes for the queen and the twelve princesses," Phoenix said. "It's almost as good as being a painter with a royal patron."

"I believe," Aunt Twisle said, "Master Snailkips also makes the dancing slippers for the Royal Dancing Company."

"I suppose he is as aristocratic as you can get," Aunt Mulgaussy said, "for a shoemaker." She sighed, placed the straw hat on her head at a jaunty angle, and seemed to melt back into the chintz chair. "Whatever shall I tell Ebbon Lloyd? He's so handsome, so dreamy. If I were only ten years younger . . ."

"Well," Aunt Twisle said slowly, "considering the dignity of Snailkips's royal appointment, I suppose it would not hurt to discuss an apprenticeship, if your heart is so set on this shoemaking business, Phoenix."

"It is! Oh, it is!" Phoenix cried, jumping up. "Please, please!"

Aunt Twisle smoothed her red ruffled dress over her knees and sighed. "Brace yourselves, Mulgaussy, Liona. We shall call on Percy Snailkips."

3

The Worn-out Shoes

A MONTH LATER, PHOENIX STOOD outside Percy Snailkips's shop washing fingerprints off the big window. "Shop" did not properly describe the six cluttered workrooms and the three apprentices, two journeymen, and master who filled them. Alfred, Whelk, and Phoenix were the apprentices; Lance and Tucker were the journeymen. Phoenix was the only girl. She was an apprentice on a trial basis—probation, the shoemaker called it. As the newest apprentice, she did the lowliest jobs, and to her dismay, none of them had anything to do with making shoes. She swept the floor; picked up endless scraps of leather, thread, and fabric; tidied and sharpened tools; ran errands; and cleaned—

"Phoenix Dance!" a voice cried behind her. "How can you wash that filthy Royalist's window!"

With the wet rag dripping in her hand, Phoenix turned and saw her friend, Rora, standing with both hands plunked against her hips. She had long, curly black hair, pulled severely back into one thick braid that hung to her waist. Her head looked sleek, like an otter's. She was fifteen.

She and Phoenix had been friends since Phoenix was nine and Rora was ten. They had met one cold day when Rora had been standing on a box in front of the Parliament Building berating the queen for not providing better schools for the poor. Phoenix, fascinated, had gone up to her and asked if she was cold and would like to have Phoenix's somewhat raggedy brown shawl. Rora had agreed at once. And after Rora had made her speech three times, she had allowed Phoenix to take her home for supper.

"I told you I was apprenticing here," Phoenix said now.

"Yes, but to learn to make fancy shoes, which is bad enough, not to wash the windows and clean that insufferable lettering. Shoemaker to the Royal Household, indeed. The Royalist boasts of it!" Rora scowled. A large mole protruded beneath her lower lip. She scraped her upper teeth over it, then added, "There are hundreds of barefoot children in this city, but the queen, the consort king, and the princesses, oh, they must be shod with beautiful, expensive shoes!" Rora's brown eyes shone against her golden brown skin. "How can you wash the windows of such a man?"

Using her thumbnail, Phoenix scraped something crusted on the glass. "You know an apprentice has to do everything," she said.

"When the Archipelago Party comes to power, the bare-foot beggar children will be shod before the princesses."

Phoenix sighed. She had heard all this before. Rora was a leader in a youth group of the Archipelago Party, called the Dolphins, which wanted less power for the monarchy and nobles and more for the people. Currently, the Parliament was made up of the House of Islands. One lord or lady from each island in the kingdom—selected by the aristocracy—represented that island's interests as the Parliament made laws for the common good. The Archipelagans wanted a second House of Parliament, with elected representatives—the House of the Archipelago.

"If all goes well, there won't be any princesses," Rora added. Always an extremist, Rora, like many in the Archipelago Party, wanted to eliminate the monarchy altogether.

"I'm holding a meeting of the Dolphins tonight at Wilburton's house," Rora said. "We're tired of talk. There's going to be some real action at last. Will you come?"

"I don't think—"

"You!" Percy Snailkips shouted, opening the door. He waved a wooden mallet at Rora. "You keep away from my shop. I know you. You're one of those Archipelagans stirring up trouble against our good queen. I won't have you bothering my workers. Get on with you."

"It's a public street," Rora said. "I've got a right to be here."

"I've finished the window, Rora," Phoenix said softly. "I

have to go in now anyway. Please, please don't cause any trouble. I'll see you later."

"Just you wait, Percy Snailkips," Rora said, "Shoemaker to the Royal Household. Soon you Royalists will be out of power, then we'll see what we'll see."

"Off with you!" roared the shoemaker, his face red. "Before I take this mallet to your backside."

Phoenix dumped her bucket of dirty water into the street, then took the bucket and rags back into the shop. Rora stayed outside with her arms crossed over her chest, staring in the window. A few minutes later, she pressed both hands against the glass, leaving smeary prints, then she spit on the glass and walked away.

"Phoenix!" Percy Snailkips scolded, shaking one of his fat fingers in her face. "I don't care who you see in your free time, though you might choose better friends. Kloud's Thunder! That one's sure to lead you into trouble. But when you're working in my shop, I don't want you talking to anyone in the Archipelago Party—unless they're customers, of course. Is that clear?"

"Yes, sir," Phoenix said. "I'm sorry. Rora just came along."

"I doubt it. That one plans every move she makes. Now go to the stove and stir the glue pot. Alfred will show you."

In the next room Alfred was standing beside the stove. He gave Phoenix the wooden spoon.

"Don't let the glue burn, beggar girl," he said. Delighted

not to be the lowliest apprentice anymore, Alfred ordered Phoenix around whenever he could.

"What's it for?" she asked. Although Phoenix had been working for only two weeks, she had already learned to ask questions whenever she could. So far, there had been few lessons; she had learned almost nothing about shoemaking. She was not allowed to touch the beautiful satins and silks, or the beads, rosettes, and ribbons. If there were no lessons, how would she ever learn to make the most beautiful shoes in the kingdom? Phoenix stirred the glue glumly. "What's it for?" she asked again.

"Just do as you're told," Alfred said.

She considered hurling a spoonful of glue at his pudgy face.

"It's for these," said Whelk, coming up beside them with a pair of finished dancing slippers in his hand. The oldest apprentice, Whelk was fifteen and handsome, though he walked with a limp. His black hair swept sideways across his forehead, slanting over his blue eyes with their faint rim of gold. Phoenix felt her heart beat a little faster whenever she spoke to him or looked at him.

"We glue on the soles, then stitch them in place," Whelk explained. "We make a hundred every month for the School of the Royal Dancers and the Royal Dancing Company."

"Oh, the Royal Dancers." Phoenix wrinkled her nose. She had once seen a group of them laughing at some street dancers who were performing on Harbor Road. Those royal dancers were so smug in their royal blue cloaks. They had everything: the best dancing slippers, fine clothes and food, money, and an opera house in which to dance. Street dancers like Phoenix's aunts had nothing. They danced in rain and wind, all for a few coins tossed in a hat. Many danced barefoot.

"These soft dancing shoes are easy enough to make," Whelk said. "Pink kid leather uppers, leather soles, drawstring around the throat. The dancers sew on the ribbons themselves. You'll be making these soon enough."

"Really?" Phoenix dropped the wooden spoon and took one of the slippers. The soft kid leather was a better quality than any her aunts had ever worn. When, oh, when would she start making shoes? She turned the slipper over and looked at the sole.

"Galgantica, of course," Whelk said. "But not the best rendering." Burned into the slipper's sole—as it was on every sole of every shoe made in Faranor—was the image of the earthshaker sea serpent Galgantica. Her body, it was said, coiled all the way around the island of Faranor. Once every hundred years, she woke and shook the island, causing great devastation. Her image was burned into every sole so that people could crush her and subdue her power with every step they took.

"I've been trying to talk the master into using a more accurate rendering," Whelk added. He held out a wooden carving hanging on a thong around his neck. "This is Galgantica, too. You see, she's got seven coils. On the slipper's sole, she has only six. But most lore masters agree she has seven. I've read about it."

"You and your sea monsters," Alfred scoffed. "He's got a whole collection of them in the back room where we sleep." Alfred and Whelk boarded with Percy Snailkips. "I think it's crazy. They give me the creeps. He's always trying to put spells on them."

"Spells?" asked Phoenix.

"I want to be a wizard," Whelk explained. "I'm saving up my money for passage on a ship to take me to the famous wizards' school on Honorath in the Eastern Reach."

"Why don't you just work your way as a deckhand?" Phoenix asked.

Whelk flushed.

"He can't do the work," Alfred said. "Not with that bum leg of his. But why do you need to go to the school at all? Why not have your uncle Fengal teach you? Isn't he a powerful wizard?"

"He is, but he won't . . . he's too busy to teach me," Whelk said. "He works with the Archipelago Party and the High Council of Wizards, and sometimes he even advises the queen."

"Can you do any magic?" Phoenix asked.

"A few simple spells. I'm reading all the books on magic I can find in the Book Tower."

"Our Whelk has lots of famous relatives," said Alfred with a sly look. "His father was Kyriad Frissian."

"The spy?" asked Phoenix. "Really?" Kyriad Frissian had been hung five years before for being a notorious spy during the war with the Peliar Kingdom to the west.

Whelk pressed his lips together, nodded once, and limped away.

"One thing I know for sure," Alfred said, handing Phoenix the wooden spoon, "that glue isn't going to get made by spying or magic or wizardry. Now stir, beggar girl! And when you're done—wash the front window again!" He grinned, triumphant.

Phoenix stirred the glue faster and faster until some sloshed out of the pot and dripped onto her new shoes. Percy Snailkips had given them to her on her first day of work. Alfred had made them, and the toes did not match. "Can't have a shoemaker's apprentice running about in holey shoes," the shoemaker had said. "Bad for business." The plain, brown, ankle-high boots were a little too big, but they kept her feet warm and dry. Aunt Mulgaussy had knitted her some thick socks to wear with them. She thought about Whelk's father. Imagine your own father being hung for high treason as a spy. She wondered if Whelk's mother was still alive.

"Phoenix!" shouted Tucker, one of the journeymen. "Didn't I tell you to sort that bin of lasts?"

"Oh, right!" Phoenix dropped the spoon into the pot. She had forgotten about the lasts—wooden molds shaped like feet. Tucker had told her to organize them by size. She rushed over to straighten the bin. She ran back and forth between the bin and the glue pot, sorting the lasts, then stirring the glue. As she worked, she hummed a little song, her heart beating fast, her muscles tense, her mind whirly.

"Don't let it burn," she sang. "Don't let it burn!"

Ever since she had started working in the shop, Phoenix had felt like a wound-up music box. Though she was tired, it took her hours to fall asleep at night, and she had to be at the shop by the time the bell in Admiral Square chimed seven. Last night Aunt Twisle had warned, "You're headed straight for one of your flighty moods." And Phoenix had not even begun making shoes yet. Think how excited she would be then! Would she ever get a chance? Or would she have to clean up after the others forever?

At least Phoenix loved everything about the shoemaker's shop. She loved the yeasty smell of leather and the patterns used for cutting out the boot and shoe sides. She loved the tools—the awls, rasps, files, punches, chisels, mallets, and knives. Best of all she loved the fine fabrics and the trimmings she was not supposed to touch. But she could have all the scraps she wanted to decorate her aunts' dancing shoes.

"It can't be!" a voice roared suddenly. It was the shoemaker. "Corns and bunions! I just delivered these shoes, and look at them! Look at them! Every single one worn to shreds!"

Phoenix ran into the other room. Percy Snailkips stood on one side of the long wooden counter; a royal messenger dressed in blue and gold stood on the other side. Spread out on the counter between them was a pile of worn-out shoes that seemed to be nothing but a collection of holes.

Phoenix remembered that yesterday these had been exquisite shoes, as lovely as anything she had ever seen in the shop window. Now, though, the velvets were worn to a shine, the satins frayed and torn. A ragged hole gaped in the toe of a shoe covered with gold brocade. Several of the shoes were missing heels. On a pair of sealskin ankle boots, the side seams had been ripped out, and half the green feathers around the top were missing. Rhinestones had popped off buckles. Rosettes of lace had rips and tears. The shoes were a sad, bedraggled lot.

"Kloud's Thunder! How could the princesses have worn the shoes to shreds in just one day?" Percy Snailkips asked the royal messenger.

"That is precisely what the Master of the Royal Wardrobe sent me here to ask you," the royal messenger said, wiggling his mustache. "The twelve princesses received their new shoes yesterday. They wore them to dinner and in the drawing room after dinner. Then they went to bed. This morning, their ladies-in-waiting found the shoes worn to tatters, as you see. Master Shoemaker, you must have used shoddy materials."

"Never!" Percy Snailkips exclaimed. "I've been the queen's shoemaker for seven years now, so I have, and I've always used the very best materials—the very finest—for Her Majesty's household. I don't understand this. But I'll replace the shoes at once." He took a deep breath. "At my own expense, of course."

"See that you do. Or you won't be keeping your royal appointment very long." And with that, the royal messenger left the shop.

The shoemaker slammed his fist on the counter; the worn-out shoes jumped. Then he shouted out orders right and left. "Alfred, clear my bench! Whelk, get out the sketches of the shoes! Tucker, get the lasts of the princesses' feet!"

Phoenix ran back to the other room to stir the glue, but it had burned on the bottom into a gooey black crust. Percy Snailkips came up behind her and peered into the pot.

"Phoenix!" he exclaimed. "I see you can't yet be trusted with the simplest task. You're still on probation, remember. Go wash your friend's mess off the window. Lance! Make up a batch of fresh glue with your own hands. All right, everyone. We have twelve pairs of shoes to make before anyone goes home tonight."

4

The Palace and the Princesses

WHEN THE CLOCK TOWER IN Admiral Square struck four hours past midnight, only Percy Snailkips and Phoenix were still awake. She had sent a note to her aunts telling them she would be spending the night at work. Alfred snored over his workbench, his lips sputtering. The others lay asleep, too, curled on benches or stretched out on the floor. Phoenix, who was not a bit sleepy, stood on the shoemaker's right-hand side watching everything he did, handing him tools when he asked and sometimes before.

"I'll say this for you, Phoenix," he said, stitching the sole onto a red velvet shoe, "you're no shirker. You look as bright and cheery as you did this morning. Where do you get so much pluck?"

"I don't know," she said. "But I've learned a lot from

watching you, the most I've learned so far—though I know watching isn't the same as doing. I can already imagine the shoes I'll make one day. They'll be the most beautiful shoes in the kingdom. Maybe for the queen herself, just wait and see, sir. I imagine white velvet quarters, with an ivory kid tongue—isn't that funny, a tongue, as though shoes can taste or something—lace ribbons, a long vamp, seed pearls around the rand between the sole and shoe, and, oh! Speaking of seed pearls, when I was little I thought they were really seeds, and you could stick one in the dirt, and it would grow into a bush with pearl necklaces and earrings and—"

"Stop! Stop!" the shoemaker cried. "I can't keep up with your chattering notions this late at night. Sometimes you do talk a lot, girlie. Leaping so fast from thought to thought a body can scarce keep up. You'll have to learn to hold your tongue when you go to the palace with me tomorrow."

"Me, sir?" Phoenix clasped the workbench. "Me, go to the palace?"

He nodded. "I always deliver shoes to the Royal Household myself—want to be sure they fit. Can't have any blisters or bunions on royal heels and toes, now can we?"

Phoenix laughed loudly. Whelk, sleeping with one hand clasped over the carving of Galgantica, stirred.

"Calm yourself, Phoenix," the shoemaker said, "or you'll wake the others."

Phoenix spread a cloak over Whelk. His cheek was pink; she wanted to stroke it, but she did not dare.

"Prepare me another boar bristle," Percy Snailkips said. "I'm almost ready for the next shoe."

Phoenix had been fascinated to learn that instead of using needles to stitch soles, shoemakers joined both ends of their thread to stiff boar bristles. She used spit to work the feathered end of a bristle into one end of the thread. Then she did the same with the other end of the thread. When that was done, she waxed the entire strand to smooth it out and make it strong. This way, there was no doubled thickness of thread to work through the hole as there would have been with a needle. The shoemaker punched all the holes with an awl before stitching them.

When Phoenix handed the shoemaker the prepared thread, he praised her. "You've learned that well enough at least."

"That's about all I've learned—except for watching you tonight. When will I be making shoes of my own, sir? I have so many ideas I long to make. Night before last when I couldn't sleep, I must have thought of ten different ideas in five minutes."

"Bit excitable, aren't you?" The shoemaker pulled both ends of the thread tight, his arms opening wide like a bird stretching its wings. "Don't fret, you'll be making shoes soon enough. Now, where was I? Oh, yes. Taking you to the palace tomorrow. Alfred usually comes, to push the handcart with the shoe boxes, but I want you to come instead. I'll teach you to fit the shoes on the royal women. It came to me the last time I was there. I thought to myself, Percy Snailkips, these royal ladies might like having a gentle female handle their feet instead of an oaf like you. Modesty and all that, you know?"

"But . . ." Phoenix glanced down at her dress. It was cheap brown kersey, too small, and had more patches than a juggler's costume. "I can't wait on the princesses dressed like this."

"Don't worry! I gave you shoes, didn't I? My daughter, Teeska, is about your age, a little older maybe. At first light, I'll send you next door to borrow a dress." The shoemaker's house adjoined the shop on the west side.

At two o'clock that afternoon, wearing a gold broadcloth dress with slits in the sleeves to show the red undertunic, Phoenix pushed the handcart with the creaky left wheel through the Palace District. She still could not believe she was going to the palace. Percy Snailkips, in a fine black suit with a double row of silver buttons, walked beside her, puffing.

Phoenix had spent little time in the Palace District, also called the Court of Canals because of all the canals crisscrossing it like a glimmering silver net. Along the banks stood mansions with carved stone façades. Some had rows of carved scallop shells above the doors, some had rows of cresting waves, still others had sea horses or starfish. Gondolas bobbed at the doors of the mansions or slipped in front of them along the canals. To ward off magic, most of the mansions had stone gargoyles perched on the roofs, their pinched, grotesque faces dark gray against the white clouds in the sky.

Phoenix and Percy Snailkips crossed a bridge over the Adamantine Canal. Beneath them, the tide rolled in, gurgling, smelling of salt, seaweed, and damp wood. The smell made Phoenix feel alive, ready for anything, even though she had not slept at all the night before. She felt as if she could run a race, climb the tallest tree, do anything and everything brilliantly.

After Phoenix and the shoemaker had crossed two more bridges, they entered an enormous courtyard with a bank of wide, flat steps at the far end. At the top of the steps, the palace of blue and violet stone rose in front of them like a dream from a fairy tale. Tower after tower soared up, the four largest at each of the four compass points—north, south, east, and west—to symbolize the monarch's dominion over every part of the kingdom. All of the towers had lacy crenellated tops made of white stone. The flags of Faranor and Windward flew from a silver dome in the center.

In spite of the dress she wore, Phoenix could not believe the guards would allow her to set foot in such a beautiful place. She followed the shoemaker through to the tradesfolk's entrance in back of the palace. There, a steward bid them wait in the tradesfolk's parlor until a footman could take them to the princesses. Even the parlor was fancier than any room Phoenix had ever seen, with carved oak tables, straight-backed chairs covered with blue upholstery, a green sofa without a single patch or tear, and striped yellow paper on the walls. Percy Snailkips fretted, patting the boxes, folding and unfolding his hands.

"These shoes are perfect," he said, his face pinched and gray with fatigue. "I'll stake my reputation on it. But I should have added one more silk orchid to Princess Pythia's shoes." He sighed. "I hope the princesses aren't too angry about the last batch."

After ten minutes, a footman led them through one ornate hallway after another, all filled with royal blue carpets and gilt-framed paintings of nobles long dead. The sound of the creaky wheel on the handcart seemed to echo off the polished chests and chairs lined up here and there along the walls. At the end of one long hallway, they approached double wooden doors carved like a mask. A footman stood stiffly beside them. When he opened one door, the mask, losing half its face, seemed to wink. Two men came out, one tall, one short, both in wizards' robes. The tall man had a black mustache, a long black beard, and black eyebrows that grew together across his nose, making him look fierce. Percy Snailkips bowed and drew back to let the men pass.

"The tall one is Whelk's uncle, Fengal," Percy Snailkips whispered to Phoenix. She recognized Fengal, whom she had seen from a distance at Archipelago Party meetings. Just after the wizards had passed, Fengal glanced back, gave Phoenix a puzzled look, and frowned. Then the two men went on.

Phoenix followed the footman into the biggest, grandest

room she had ever seen. Scattered around it, sitting on velvet sofas and tapestry chairs, were the twelve princesses.

Two sat on a bench before a harpsichord, but their fingers did not touch the ivory keys. A third sat beside a golden harp, but she did not touch the strings. The fourth, fifth, and sixth sat beside embroidery frames; instead of holding needles, however, they clasped their hands in their laps. The seventh princess stared at two golden balls in her hand. The eighth, dressed in dove-colored gray, stood alone before an easel, though she held no brush. She looked out the window; her profile seemed carved in stone. Beside her crouched a stuffed leopard that seemed about to spring; the princess had her hand upon its head. The other four princesses held closed books. On the tables were cups of tea that had not been drunk, plates of cookies that had not been eaten. The princesses were as still as statues, the room as silent as a tomb. Phoenix wondered what was wrong with them.

"Your Royal Highnesses," said the footman, "the master shoemaker has arrived."

Instantly, the room came alive. The princesses left the silent harp and harpsichord, left their chairs, left their needlework frames and their closed books and their cups of cold tea, and rushed up to the shoemaker and Phoenix. They crowded in too close. Phoenix stepped back.

"At last!" said the princess in the gown of dove gray, who appeared to be the eldest. "Master Shoemaker, we thought you would never arrive. Praised be the Sea Maid that you are here at last."

"At your service, Princess Aurantica." The shoemaker bowed.

Phoenix curtsied to the floor and almost fell over, so awed was she to be in the presence of the crown princess, heir to the throne of Windward.

"The shoes! Have you brought them?" cried another princess, her voice hard and shrill. "Oh, please, have you brought them? Where are they?" She was the littlest, dressed like a daffodil in yellow frills. Unfortunately, the color made her sallow skin look even more sallow.

Phoenix noticed that every one of the princesses' dresses was a different color. Did they consult with each other about their clothes every morning? What happened if two of the princesses wanted to wear pink on the same day?

"The shoes!" the littlest princess said again. "We must have them, you know. We have got to have them. Oh, please, hurry."

"Patience, Princess Batissa," the shoemaker said. Batissa, Phoenix knew, was the youngest princess, thirteen years old. "If Your Highnesses would be so good as to be seated," the shoemaker added, "my new apprentice and I will fit the shoes. I beg your patience while I instruct her. Will you all speak your names to her?"

The princesses introduced themselves to Phoenix: Aurantica, Myadora, Semele, Engina, Pythia, Tigrina and Lucina—the twins—Osea, Coral, Natica and Norris—the second set of twins—and last, Batissa. All twelve princesses were named after seashells, some found only on the holy island of Alamora. As they settled themselves on the sofas and chairs and their ladies-in-waiting began removing the princesses' white kid slippers, which were full of holes, Phoenix stared up at the ceiling. It was painted like the sea. In a swirl of blue waves tipped with white foam were sailing ships, treasure chests, writhing sea monsters, and pearl-bedecked mermaids with shiny silver tails.

"It is a lovely painting, isn't it?" asked Princess Aurantica. "Though the chiaroscuro technique is a bit flawed. I wish I could do so well myself."

"You're a painter, Your Highness?" Phoenix asked, glancing at the easel. On it was a painting of a dragon spewing an enormous flame, with small figures dancing around it in wild abandon.

"I am. But unfortunately, no one takes me seriously."

"What do you mean?"

"Because I am a princess, and expected to rule one day, everyone believes I am just playing at being a painter. For example, I asked to apprentice with the great Leonarth. He smiled, bowed, gave me a corner in his studio away from everything. He praised me and left me alone. Gave me no criticism, no attention. How could I learn? To him I was a princess playing, wasting his time."

"Oh," said Phoenix, not knowing what else to say.

"Enough of this!" Princess Coral, who had long red hair coiled up in a bun on her head, stood up and slapped the top box on the handcart. "Are you going to talk all day or will we ever see the shoes?"

Phoenix looked at her, surprised by the desperate expression on her face. The princess let out a sob, then quickly put her hand to her mouth to stifle it.

"Yes," said Princess Semele, her green eyes somber. "Night comes soon, and we must be ready. Oh, please let us have the shoes."

"We are sorry to be so insistent, Master Shoemaker," Princess Norris said. Her cheeks were as pink as her dress. "But please understand that it is imperative for us to have the shoes. Give them to us now, now! Do not be cruel and keep them from us. We beg you."

"Of course," Percy Snailkips said, "of course. You shall have them at once. Unload the handcart please, Phoenix."

Phoenix, wondering why the princesses were so desperate to get their shoes, untied the string that secured the shoe boxes and passed them to the shoemaker. On the top of each box, written in flowing script, was a name. The shoemaker placed one box beside the feet of each princess.

"Now," he said, "if you will wait, I will make my way to each of you in turn starting with the eldest—" But the princesses grabbed the boxes, ripped off the lids, tore off the protective muslin, and slid their feet into the shoes.

Then they rose and began to dance, each alone. The princesses moved with exquisite grace in steps that were stately, heavy, and measured—arms arching over heads, toes pointed, necks curved. The grandeur and sadness of their movements made Phoenix's heart ache. They made her want to cry. From the moment she had come into their room, the princesses had made her want to cry. Instead of crying, however, something snapped inside her and Phoenix began to laugh.

"Phoenix," the shoemaker whispered, "get ahold of yourself!"

But Phoenix laughed harder and harder until she doubled over, clutching her stomach. Some of it was tiredness, she knew, and some of it was the music-box feeling of being wound up too tightly.

Suddenly, as though in response to Phoenix's laughter, the princesses' dancing changed. It grew faster and more frenetic as they began to twirl and leap wildly around the room. Then they began to laugh, too, their voices piercing and brittle.

To Phoenix everything seemed hilarious, even the silver buttons wiggling on the shoemaker's jacket as he huffed and puffed. It seemed as though she and the princesses were in league against the ladies-in-waiting and the shoemaker, who were trying vainly to calm them down.

"What is your name?" cried Princess Lucina. "Who is this jolly apprentice who knows how to amuse us?"

"I'm Phoenix!" she gasped. "Phoenix Dance of Trebonness."

"A girl in a gold and red dress," said Princess Osea,

known for her book learning. "Yes, she's a phoenix indeed! A firebird rising from ashes to flame. Straight out of the myth."

When at last the ladies-in-waiting had calmed the princesses down, Percy Snailkips began to check the fit of each pair of shoes. Phoenix stood beside him and watched.

"See, Phoenix, the heel must not slip out," he said. "So. How does that feel, Princess Aurantica? Good, good. And across the toe joints, the shoe must not pinch. Just so, Princess Myadora." And on down the line he went in order of age until he reached Princess Batissa.

"At last," she said, stroking the blue feather on her left shoe. "They are lovely. I shall never take them off."

"Your dress is beautiful," Phoenix told her. "You look like spring."

"I beg your pardon," Princess Batissa said, "but I look yellow and sallow. You see, being the youngest, I have the last choice of color each morning. And all the others look terrible in yellow, too, except Semele. But she prefers orange. She says it helps her concentrate. She's a juggler, you see."

Then Princess Batissa, tipping her head first to the right and then to the left, pointed at Phoenix. "Something is wrong with you," she said.

"What do you mean?" Phoenix asked.

"My sister has premonitions," Princess Osea explained. "And she does not know when to hold her tongue."

"Why should I?" Princess Batissa said. "I am often right, aren't I?"

All the princesses nodded.

"Once," said Princess Norris, "Batissa had a premonition that one of us would have a terrible accident. The next day, my sister Natica was thrown from her horse."

"Another time," Princess Lucina said, "Batissa felt that a thief had come amongst us. It turned out that one of our ladies-in-waiting had stolen my pearl necklace."

"She is often wrong, of course," said Princess Aurantica. "Do not make yourself uneasy, Phoenix."

But Phoenix found that her hands were cold. Was something wrong with her? And if so, what?

"Well." Percy Snailkips cleared his throat, bowed, and said, "I trust these shoes will wear better than the last ones, Your Highnesses. I am sorry for the inconvenience. The fault was all mine."

In the sudden silence, the princesses all looked at each other.

"But . . ." Princess Batissa began, "it wasn't your—"

"Hush, Batissa!" Princess Aurantica interrupted. Then she turned to Percy Snailkips. "We appreciate your efforts, Master Shoemaker. The shoes are lovely. We are certain they will last. Thank you for replacing the worn-out shoes so quickly."

The shoemaker bowed again. Phoenix curtsied, and they left. As soon as they reached the shop, the shoemaker scolded Phoenix for her behavior at the palace and then sent her home to sleep for the rest of the day. However, Phoenix did not even try to sleep; too many thoughts crowded in her mind as she paced back and forth in front of the curio cabinet. A little niggling pain started in the center of her chest. When her aunts came home, she began to talk rapidly.

"I went to see the princesses at the palace," she told them. "Batissa was all in yellow, Aurantica in gray. And there was a leopard—a stuffed leopard in their sitting room! It gave me the shivers! Why would they have such a thing? I kept waiting for it to pounce. The princesses were like wild animals themselves when they ripped open the boxes to get at the shoes. They were desperate to get them. I wonder why? Then they all started dancing—they're lovely dancers, very fine—especially Norris and Natica. But beautiful and sad, too, dreadfully sad. I bet they would have danced all night if the ladies-in-waiting hadn't made them stop. But at first the princesses were so still and cold, that is until they found out it was Percy Snailkips bringing the shoes. Then, well! Night and day. They must love shoes! Did you know the princesses have six inches of lace on their petticoats? Six inches! I saw it when they pulled up their dresses to try on their shoes. One of the ladies-in-waiting had a mustache. It was so funny! They had sea monsters painted on their ceiling—can you imagine? I saw the loveliest teapot with violets painted on it. One of the princesses, I think it was Osea, wore a violet-colored dress that matched her eyes and—"

"Stop! Phoenix, stop talking this instant!" Aunt Twisle cried.

But Phoenix only laughed, and as she began to tell them how she had hysterics with the princesses, her aunts stared at her with worried faces because she could not stop talking, could not stop laughing . . .

5

The Contest

THAT NIGHT, PHOENIX LAY IN HER BED on the parlor sofa, her eyes wide open, listening to the tower clock in the market strike three hours past midnight. Her pillow felt scratchy and hot against her cheek. When the third bell faded, she sat up and threw back the quilt, furious. Why couldn't she sleep? She had not slept at all the night before, and she was exhausted. Sleep seemed like a huge many-armed beast that she wrestled with but could not subdue.

Phoenix got up and tiptoed past the curio cabinet, where the skulls of the lemur and parrot gleamed in the patch of moonlight glaring through the window. She closed the door to her aunts' bedchamber to keep from waking them. In the kitchen, she poured a glass of water from the cracked blue pitcher and paced while she drank it. Then, almost crying from exhaustion and frustration, Phoenix again tried to sleep.

The next thing she knew, the tower clock was striking six. After she dressed, Phoenix lit the fire lying ready in the stove and started oatmeal for breakfast. She was tired, and yet she was not tired. Her body felt as though bees were buzzing inside it. Her chest felt tight, as though a giant fist were squeezing it. Phoenix had felt this way many times before, and she knew it meant her body and mind were working up to a feverish pitch, to one of her fiery, flighty moods. She loved these moods—before they grew too frenzied. But she did not tell her aunts.

Later that morning, her chest still hurt as Whelk taught her how to sew together the various parts of a silk shoe he had cut out. She sewed the quarters—the sides of the shoe—to the vamp, the long front of the shoe. Phoenix liked Whelk because he was the only one who took the time to teach her things, and also because he was handsome. Would his fine black hair feel as smooth as the green silk beneath her fingers?

"I can't believe I'm really touching silk at last!" she said. "I can't, can't believe it! It's wonderful, it's—"

"Keep the tension even on the thread," Whelk said. "You're pulling the stitches too tight. Loosen up a little, but . . . no, keep the stitches all the same length. You're not concentrating, Phoenix. What's the matter with you today? You look tired."

"In Kloud's Name!" they heard the shoemaker shout. "I don't believe it!"

"What now?" Phoenix asked. She and Whelk ran into the main room of the shop in time to see the royal messenger stride forward, open his sack, and dump the shoes—the ones they had all labored over the night before last—onto the counter. Phoenix crept closer to look. All the silk orchids were missing from Princess Pythia's orchid slippers. The red velvet bows dangled from the red velvet shoes, all scuffed and torn. Every single pair of shoes had holes in either the toes or the heels. All were ruined. Percy Snailkips stood there with the look of a ruined man.

"Stoven and sunk!" he exclaimed. "This cannot be!"

"The evidence speaks for itself," the royal messenger said. "As before, the princesses wore these shoes only to dinner and in the drawing room afterward. This morning, their ladies-in-waiting found the shoes in tatters, as you see, Master Shoemaker."

"Then the princesses must be sneaking out of their bedchamber!" the shoemaker roared. "They must be wearing the shoes during the night!"

"How dare you accuse them of disobedience and deceit," the royal messenger said. "Besides, the princesses' bedchamber is guarded. The guards have sworn the princesses never left their room during the night."

"Then they must be dancing inside their bedchamber all night long!" the shoemaker exclaimed.

"The guards heard no sound coming from the princesses' room. And they look in on the princesses each time the clock strikes the hour. They are always sleeping soundly in their beds. You must own up to this, Master Shoemaker—the fault is yours." The steward unrolled a piece of parchment, cleared his throat, and read: "By command of Her Majesty, Queen Zandora of Windward, Percy Snailkips the master shoemaker is regrettably hereby relieved of his appointment as Shoemaker to the Royal Household. Because no fault has been found with the shoes he makes for the Royal Dancers, he may continue to hold that post by the queen's favor. Signed Lord Thorpe, Master of the Royal Wardrobe for Her Majesty, Queen Zandora of the Royal House of Seaborne." The royal messenger rolled up the parchment, whacked it sharply against his palm, and left.

Percy Snailkips sank down in a chair and put his head in his hands. The others tiptoed around, returning to their tasks. No one said a word. Whelk stroked the sea monster hanging around his neck—today Halgerblath, the giant squid, said to sink ships with a single blow from one of his eighteen arms.

"Wearing out their shoes in one night," Whelk said. "I smell magic. I bet there's wizardry at work here. Maybe even the Order of the Black Dragon."

Phoenix shivered. She had heard of the Order of the Black Dragon. It was a secret group of dark wizards who used their power to wreak havoc throughout Windward. Their goal was to take over the kingdom and rule it themselves. The queen used good wizards, like Whelk's uncle Fengal and the High Council of Wizards, to fight against them.

Phoenix went to the stove, made a pot of tea, poured a cup, and took it to the shoemaker, who had not moved.

"Thank you, Phoenix," he said.

"Is it so very bad, sir?" she asked. "I mean, you still have lots of other customers. Nobles and other rich folks who want your shoes."

The shoemaker shook his head. "Once they hear the queen has taken away my royal appointment, they'll know I'm out of favor. They'll take their trade to whatever shoemaker she favors next—to be in fashion. But where? That's what I'd like to know. Where will the queen go for her shoes now? To Master Kilwarren? Bah! Mistress Odark? Hmph! There's no better shoemaker in Faranor than I! It's not pride nor vanity speaking; it's plain truth. There wasn't a thing wrong with those shoes!"

"Then something must be wrong with the princesses," Phoenix said. She remembered how unnaturally still the princesses had been when she and the shoemaker had first entered their room. Then she remembered how eagerly they had torn open the boxes of shoes, how brightly their eyes had glittered, how sadly and wildly they had danced.

"Aye." The shoemaker sighed. "And that's what troubles me most. What is wrong with our princesses?"

The day after the next was blustery, the fifteenth day in the month of Cloudburst. At three o'clock—Percy Snailkips let his workers off early on Landays—Phoenix paced through

Sea Dragon Courtyard while Rora followed behind her, passing out pamphlets about the Archipelago Party. Phoenix's aunts danced with the Seven Sea Stars in front of the fountain. The wind whipped the water into a white spray around the bronze sea dragon, which looked like a monster emerging from the deep. Leaves skittered through the courtyard, leaves and bits of paper and a red hair ribbon that some girl had dropped. Phoenix, unable to break her old habit of collecting scraps, chased the red ribbon. When she caught it, she put it in her pocket and walked on.

At the end of the courtyard, Phoenix turned and started skipping here and there. She could not stay still. The pain in her chest was back, sharper now. She had slept poorly again last night, and the bees buzzing inside her were growing more frantic. Thoughts flew through her mind like flashes of bright color—thoughts about Whelk, thoughts about the worn-out shoes, thoughts about what might be wrong with the princesses, and thoughts about the shoes she would never have the chance to make for them now.

When Phoenix was halfway back across the courtyard, she heard hammering and turned to look. Across the street, a boy in royal livery was nailing a parchment onto the wall of an apothecary's shop.

"A proclamation?" Rora wondered, catching up to her.

"Let's go see," Phoenix said. They crossed the street, dodging carriages and carts, pushed their way to the front of the crowd, and read the proclamation.

Her Majesty Queen Zandora announces a contest for the appointment of Shoemaker to the Royal Household. Anyone may enter. All contestants must submit two pairs of sample shoes, one for the eldest princess, Her Royal Highness Crown Princess Aurantica, and one for the youngest princess, Her Royal Highness Princess Batissa. The shoes must be submitted to the Master of the Royal Wardrobe by the thirtieth day of the month of Cloudburst. The winner will be named Shoemaker to the Royal Household and will receive a royal appointment.

"Honestly," Rora said. "Doesn't the queen have more important things to worry about?"

Phoenix's heart beat fast. Her thoughts began to spin, concocting designs of shoes. She pictured one design after another—each more fantastic and beautiful than the last. Of course she would enter the contest; she had to enter. But would Percy Snailkips allow it? She would beg him to let her use the materials in the shop and the lasts of the princesses' feet. Phoenix could not use scraps for these shoes. If she won, she would bring trade and honor back to the shop. For a moment, Phoenix saw herself as Shoemaker to the Royal Household—the most important shoemaker in the kingdom!

Rora was watching her. "You're going to enter, aren't you? You're hopeless. Wilburton and the others in the Dolphins are right. Your aunt Mulgaussy has too much influence over you. You're practically a Royalist!" She slid her front teeth down over the mole beneath her lower lip and wiggled it. "Why don't you spend your time doing something useful, like coming to our meetings? There's one tonight. An important one. We're meeting at nine o'clock at Tarim's house. Promise you'll come and prove to everyone you're not a Royalist."

"All right, all right! I'll come. But I have to go and talk to my aunts now."

Phoenix's aunts were just finishing a dance called *The Tale of the Mermen*, performed to the music of a viol. As the seven dancers took their last pose, applause rang through the courtyard. The dancers bowed. Coins flashed and jingled into the black velvet top hat they passed. After the troupe had divided the money, Phoenix rushed up to her aunts and told them about the contest.

"I will make shoes dripping with pearls," Phoenix cried. "For Aurantica, crown princess, they will be regal, as befits a future queen. And for Batissa, something like a butterfly, something light and gay, with feathers. Ribbons. All frothy. Or perhaps clogs for Aurantica, to raise her feet from the muddy road. All in silver, with silver cording and beads. Or perhaps—oh, this would be splendid—I'll have a scene from Windward's history painted on the finest leather. Maybe the first meeting of the God and Goddess, Kloud and Nemaree. Or their daughter, the Sea Maid, riding the waves on her scallop shell. There'll be lots of foam! And dolphins! All glittery bright with sparkles, maybe bangles and—"

"Really, Phoenix!" cried Aunt Twisle. "This excited mood of yours has gone on for days now. It's getting worse and worse. I don't think we can allow you to enter this contest. It'll make you even more excited."

"You've hardly slept a wink," said Aunt Liona, untying her dancing shoes. "And you talk all the time. Talk, talk, talk."

"And you're irritable and jumpy," Aunt Mulgaussy said. "The great-granddaughter of Seagraine Dance should be gracious and—"

"A blight on Seagraine Dance!" Phoenix exclaimed. "I'm fine! I just have ideas! So many lovely ideas. What's wrong with that? Oh, please, dear Aunt Twisle. Let me enter! Please? I promise I'll sleep. I'll be calm. I'll be as calm as a still sea. As calm as a lake without wind. Calm, calm, calm, unruffled, sleeping like a baby, sleeping like Galgantica . . . I must enter. How can you think of not letting me enter? You wouldn't be so cruel!" Suddenly, Phoenix was furious. Her aunts seemed like three looming giants trying to keep her from her greatest dream.

"I don't care what you say," Phoenix shouted, "I'm going to enter! And I'm going over to Percy Snailkips's house right now and see if he'll let me use materials from the shop." Without waiting for permission, Phoenix ran across the courtyard. She plunged onto Harbor Road, where a horse and wagon nearly ran over her.

"Look out there, fool girl!" the driver cried. "Trying to get yourself killed?"

Phoenix felt her blood pounding as she skittered out of

the way. She would show her aunts, she would show them! She would be Shoemaker to the Royal Household. As she ran down Harbor Road, the spicy smell of sausages frying in a vendor's stall went straight to her brain, and never, never had she smelled anything so delicious. Phoenix wanted to gobble ten of them without stopping. A woman selling flowers had baskets stuffed with early blooming cherry blossoms that were so pink and delicate and exquisite that Phoenix almost cried out for joy. They smelled of spring, and she wanted to grab a bunch and dance down the street with them, scattering them as she went, her skirt whirling amid showers of pink petals. She was certain they were a sign that she would win the contest—the contest! The wonderful, wonderful contest! Could she make cherry blossom shoes for Princess Batissa? All shimmering in pink, silver, and white?

The wind blasted against Phoenix's face, and she laughed, delighted, wishing it would blow harder. She wanted to climb onto the back of the wind and dance until she grew dizzy. She pulled out the red ribbon and held it high over her head so that it trailed behind her as she ran down the street. With every step she took, with everything she saw, smelled, touched, and delighted in, the stabbing pain inside her chest grew sharper. A fire seemed to burn inside her.

Percy Snailkips stood at his open door while she told him about the contest.

"Slow down, Phoenix," he said. "You're gabbling. I cannot understand a word."

She tried again, drawing the red ribbon through her fingers over and over as she talked.

"Oh, a contest," he said. "Why are you bothering me about this at home? At this hour right before supper? Am I to have no peace anywhere?"

"Oh, please, I couldn't wait," Phoenix said. "I had to know. Will you let me enter? Will you? Oh, please, please? I'll wash the shop window ten times a day and never complain if you'll just let me enter!"

"You won't be able to use expensive materials—no pearls or golden threads or whatever it is I see you're dreaming of. I can't afford it. I can barely keep and feed all my workers, now I've lost the royal appointment. And you'll be up against it, Phoenix. Other shoemakers will spare no expense to get this appointment. They'll put their life savings into costly materials. I don't see how you can compete with that."

"I can. I must. I will!"

"And your skills, well . . ." He ran one hand over his chin. "You don't know anything yet. I doubt you can make whatever ideas are bubbling in that head of yours."

"I'll ask questions. I've a shop full of shoemakers who can help me. Won't you help? Please say I can enter. Please? Please?"

"Well, if you're that determined." He shrugged. "I guess there's no harm in it."

Phoenix hugged him round his fat middle. "Thank you! Thank you! I'll bring the trade back to the shop and make you proud. You'll see. Everyone will see!" And she ran off toward home, one hand pressed against her aching chest. She looked up at the sky. As the late winter day drew to a close, the fiery red sunset blazing across the western sky was edged with darkness.

6

A Hammer in the Dark

YOU SAID WE WERE GOING TO A MEET-ing, Rora," Phoenix whispered later that night. She stood outside the Parliament Building peering around Rora's shoulder into the darkness. They were both pressed against the side of the building, and Phoenix could feel the edge of a stone digging into her shoulder. The night air, stirred by a faint breeze, was cool under the three-quarter moon. "I told my aunts I was going to a meeting of the Dolphins," she added.

"It is a meeting," Rora whispered. "A meeting where we finally do something. We're tired of waiting for change while the adults do nothing but talk. The Dolphins have decided to act."

"So why are we sneaking around in the dark, in dark clothes?"

"Don't you trust me?"

"Of course. You're my best friend."

"We planned it all at Wilburton's the other night," Rora said. "When you were too busy thinking about making frivolous shoes to come. It's time you proved to the others and me that you really are an Archipelagan and not a Royalist. All this talk of making shoes for the princesses—I'm not the only one who's wondering where your loyalties lie." Rora paused. "There. Tarim's waving. That's the signal. Let's go. Remember, I'm counting on you."

"For what?" Phoenix asked. "Why won't you tell me?" She was excited, however—awake and alive with the bees buzzing inside her—and she followed Rora around the corner of the building willingly enough. As they entered the courtyard in front of the Parliament Building, their footsteps tapped on the cobblestones. Huge stone urns holding bushes clipped into the shapes of animals loomed up like sentinels in the darkness. Phoenix made out a bear, a swan, a lion, and a deer.

Rora stopped in the center of the courtyard beside a statue of the twelve princesses. Each one represented a different grace—loyalty, justice, truth, love, humility, harmony, mercy, and so on. As Phoenix looked up at the marble princesses against the night sky, they seemed crowned with the blazing stars, queens of the night. She recognized Aurantica, Osea, Tigrina and Lucina, Batissa, and all the others. The likenesses were remarkable. At the base of the statue, Phoenix knew from having been there before, chiseled words said, "Protectors of the People."

Five figures clad in dark clothes approached from the opposite side of the courtyard. Two of them carried a ladder; the others carried brushes and pails of paint. After they arrived at the statue, everything began to happen fast. Three people started painting words around the base of the statue, their brushes slashing back and forth. "Join the Archipelago Party," Phoenix read. Then Wilburton, a tall boy with a long skinny neck that shone white in the moonlight, thrust a pail of paint and a brush into Phoenix's hands and whispered to her to paint "Put power in the hands of the people."

But Phoenix did not move. A stone seemed to settle in the pit of her stomach, holding her down. The brush trembled in her hand. She watched the two people carrying the ladder raise it against the statue. The white marble glimmered faintly, the stone faces of the princesses watching Rora climb up the ladder. She reached into her cloak pocket, pulled out a hammer, and slammed it against Princess Aurantica's face. Part of the nose flew off.

"Rora!" Phoenix cried. "No!"

"Be quiet!" someone exclaimed.

Rora slammed the hammer against the face of the next princess and then the next, raining blows as far as she could reach. The sound rang through the courtyard and echoed off the cobblestones. Phoenix dropped the pail of paint; it spilled, and the dark liquid bled onto the cobblestones. She took one step back, then another and another. Then she turned and ran.

"Coward!" someone yelled. "She runs!"

When Phoenix reached the edge of the Parliament Building, she slipped around the other side and darted behind a rhododendron bush. She stood with her cheek pressed against the building, panting hard. She could hear the hammer ringing and smashing, and she cringed, thinking of the princesses. Then, from the opposite direction, she heard the sound of feet running toward her. Voices shouted. Whistles blew. Phoenix shrank back as four people ran past her hiding place and into the courtyard beyond.

"Stop there!" they ordered. "What are you doing? Stop at once!"

Phoenix peered around the corner.

"Guards!" Wilburton roared. The painters dropped their pails and brushes and scattered.

"Leave the ladder," someone shouted. "Run!"

Rora jumped down. One of the guards caught her. Rora kicked and fought, swinging the hammer. Then a second guard ran up, and they pinned her arms behind her back.

"Filthy Royalists!" she screamed. "Let me go!"

Phoenix turned and ran away through the streets as fast as she could. Was there paint on her clothes? If a guard stopped her, would he know where she had been? She realized she was still clutching the paintbrush and dropped it. Soon she was lost, in a part of the city she did not know well. Buildings reared up in the darkness. Here and there, a street lantern cast a cone of ghostly light over a banister or doorway. Around every corner, she expected to see a guard waiting to pounce on her. She ran past a man in a dark cloak who turned toward her, calling, "Hello, girl," and something else she did not wait to hear.

Phoenix reached a canal. As she ran over a bridge, she felt she was suspended over nothing, and that nothing held her, and that she would drop and fall forever. She followed one canal after another but was lost in a maze and could not find her way out. The princesses' smashed faces haunted her. They were faceless now, mere stumps of stone. It seemed as though Rora had really killed them with her ringing blows, and Phoenix felt her stomach heaving and thought she might be sick. She kept running, running away from the terrible destructive power of the swinging hammer.

Then, as she turned a corner, Phoenix heard singing. She ran toward three children huddled around a fire blazing in a metal barrel. The flames leaped, curling into the darkness against the black canal water. The children were singing.

"The sailors could not flee nor fight
The power of the stormy blast.
Red tongues of fire ran up the mast
And waves of mighty breadth and height.

"The ship hit the rock and broke in half,
As mermaids swimming came and laughed,
And led the sailors to their kingdom in the sea, the sea,
To their kingdom in the sea."

The children beckoned to her. The warmth of the fire was tempting, and Phoenix stopped.

"Can you tell me the way to Harbor Road?" she asked, warming her hands beside the flames. The fire smelled of pitch and old bones.

"She's lost," said a brown-haired boy with a squint.

"She has a home to be lost from," said a little girl in a moth-eaten fur coat. "Lucky thing."

"Come sing with us," said a tall boy.

"Don't we sing pretty?" asked the little girl.

"Yes," Phoenix said, "but I must get home. Can you give me directions to Sea Dragon Courtyard?"

"Sea dragons, is it?" said the tall boy. "You've got to swim deep to find them."

"A dragon breathes fire," said the squint-eyed boy. "Like a shooting star. It will singe the flesh from your bones."

"Too much fire can kill," said the tall boy.

"If you dance around it like a wild thing," said the little girl, pointing to the barrel, "it will swallow your soul."

"Thank you. Goodbye," said Phoenix, seeing they would be no help, and she ran on. When she heard them singing again, part of her wanted to go back and sing with them around the fire while the dark water flowed by. At least it was a place. At least it was somewhere that was not lost. She saw the princesses' smashed faces again. Without their faces, it seemed to Phoenix that they, too, were lost. Then she saw Rora swinging the hammer, struggling with the guards.

Where was Rora now? What was happening to Rora? Phoenix put one hand to her mouth and muffled a sob.

At last Phoenix found a road she recognized, and from there she made her way to Harbor Road and then to Black Diamond Lane. The clock in the market was striking midnight when she opened the orange door. Her aunts were sitting in a row on the sofa, waiting, their faces pale. Aunt Mulgaussy had her knitting piled in her lap.

"Phoenix!" they exclaimed, jumping up, all talking at once.

"Where have you been?"

"Do you know what time it is?"

"This would never happen in Trebonness!"

Phoenix threw herself into Aunt Twisle's arms and sobbed, "Rora! I think Rora's been arrested!"

7

A Frenzy of Shoes

AFTER LUNCH THE NEXT DAY, Phoenix swept the shop as though she were a tornado whirling through the rooms. She delved into corners, sweeping out cobwebs, spiders, and bits of thread. She yanked out baskets of tools sitting on the floor and swept behind them. She jabbed the broom into the narrow space between the wall and the bin of lasts, making dust arc up in a speckled cloud. As she wrestled with the dirt, she thought of Rora wrestling with the guards. Phoenix tightened her grasp on the broom and swept faster, to keep from crying.

Last night, after Phoenix had told her aunts what had happened at the Parliament Building, Aunt Twisle had gone to alert Rora's parents. Phoenix had spent the rest of the night awake, worrying and crying, pacing the parlor, waiting for Aunt Twisle to come home with news. However, she had not returned before Phoenix had to leave for work.

Phoenix was dumping a dustpan full of sweepings into a pail when a mop-headed boy pushed open the shop door.

"I got a note," he said, holding out a slightly crumpled piece of paper folded into thirds. "I'm supposed to deliver it to a girl who's supposed to work here. Name of Dance. Phoenix Dance or some such strange name like that."

"That's me," Phoenix said, taking the note. "Thanks." She leaned the dustpan against the wall and glanced at the seal, which had an image of a grinning cat punched into the red wax—Aunt Twisle's seal. Phoenix broke the seal, unfolded the note, and read it.

Dear Phoenix,

I'm sorry I didn't come home last night. I know you must be anxious for news. But I stayed to watch over Rora's little brothers and sisters while her parents went to see about her. They were gone all night and have only just returned.

I'm afraid your suspicions were correct. Rora was arrested and charged with destroying public property and sedition. She's in Five Towers Prison. Her parents are doing everything they can to get her out. Don't worry. Remember, don't tell anyone you were there. I'll see you after work. Aunt Liona is making sausages to cheer us all up.

Much love,
Aunt Twisle

Percy Snailkips shepherded a customer—a lady wearing an enormous hat stitched with purple ostrich feathers—out the door. Then he turned and saw Phoenix holding the letter.

"Everything all right, Phoenix?" he asked.

"No," she said, folding the note and tucking it in her skirt pocket beneath her leather apron. She wondered if the prison officials would let her visit Rora. "My friend Rora's been arrested."

"What for?"

"For smashing that statue of the princesses in Parliament Square."

"Kloud's Thunder!" the shoemaker exclaimed. "I knew she was trouble. They ought to lock her up and throw away—" He stopped. "There, there now, don't cry." He patted Phoenix awkwardly on the back.

"I'm worried!" Phoenix cried. "What's going to happen to her? What will the guards do to her? How long will she be in prison? I can't bear to think of her in prison. She's probably lonely and scared and . . ." Phoenix picked up the broom and started sweeping again where she had already swept.

"Of course you're worried about her," Percy Snailkips said, "but there's nothing you can do. I'm sure everything will be all right. She's young. They'll probably let her off easy—a slap on the wrist. Don't worry so! Why don't you do some designs for your shoes for the contest? That'll take your mind off your troubles for a while."

Phoenix nodded. A few minutes later she was sitting at her workbench holding a bit of charcoal in her fingers. The shoemaker kept paper, charcoal, and colored chalks for drawing shoe designs. Phoenix felt so many ideas crowding into her mind that she did not know where to begin.

She drew a long, curving line. She loved the feeling of the charcoal gliding across the paper, loved the slight hissing sound it made. The line quickly turned into a pair of shoes cut low at the throat and sides, with straps called latchets fastening across the insteps. Over the latchets, Phoenix sketched lace bows. Next, she took a stick of red chalk and made the sides of the shoes red, imagining satin. With a pale gray stick, she colored the lace bows silver, then added silver tongues sweeping up behind them. The pointed toes curved slightly at the tips, like the prow of a ship—this was the current fashion.

Drawing a little faster, Phoenix made the second pair of shoes midnight blue leather. A large floral cutout design at the toe showed magenta silk beneath. On the side of the third pair of shoes, Phoenix drew the Sea Maid's face with many tiny dots, imitating sequins. The Sea Maid's face made her think of Rora swinging the hammer against the princesses' faces. Phoenix hunched her shoulders.

How could Rora have put the members of the Dolphins in such danger? Rora was always like a bomb about to explode, and she had finally exploded, and for what? What had she hoped to gain for the Archipelago Party by destroying a statue of the princesses? How would that bring the people more power? Phoenix's hand froze, holding a stick of blue chalk in midair. Would Rora tell the officials that Phoenix had been part of the group? Would she, too, be arrested and locked in Five Towers Prison with murderers and thieves? Phoenix shuddered and put down the chalk.

She took a fresh piece of paper and drew another pair of shoes, then another and another. She sketched faster and faster, her fingers unable to keep up with the rush of ideas clamoring to get out. When she picked up a red-orange stick, she thought of the glowing red-orange faces of the three children around the burn barrel, and flames seemed to burn inside her as the pictures of shoes came crowding into her head and out through her fingers. One idea suggested another, which leaped to another, like a cascading waterfall leaping from rock to rock, sweeping her along in its powerful stream. She felt ablaze with light, drunk on ideas— ecstatic, possessed, seized. She loved how she felt. She was fire and she was water, burning and surging, glowing and roaring. All the many nights of sleeplessness and the days of being wound up like a music box had driven her to this frenzy.

At three o'clock, she pinned all her sketches on the wall and went to beg the shoemaker for more paper.

"What!" Percy Snailkips roared. "You used up that whole stack? Do you have any idea how expensive paper is? You should have needed only four or five sheets at most!"

He strode to her workbench in the side room. Whelk was already there, staring at the wall, which was covered with thirty-four sketches. Percy Snailkips stopped short, and he, too, stared at the wall.

"You did all these this afternoon?" he asked, scratching his head.

"Yes, but are they good enough?" Phoenix asked. She plucked at her leather apron, her hands blackened with charcoal as though they had been burned. "I don't see one that's just right. Maybe there's something better I haven't thought of yet." She slumped down on her workbench and put one hand to her chest, trying to quiet the fiery pain. Her throat was dry. She picked up a cup on her workbench to take a drink, but it was empty.

"These are good," the shoemaker said slowly. "I knew you had ideas in that crowded head of yours, but some of these are really fine. Original. Your drawing is a little crude—only lack of experience that—but the colors and themes of each pair, you've got something here. Talent. Your aunts were right about you."

"I never would have thought of using sequins to make a face," said Whelk, pointing to the sketch of the Sea Maid.

"But which two for the princesses?" Phoenix asked. "For the contest?"

"Most of these you can't afford to make," said the shoemaker, "or rather, I can't afford to let you make them, good as they are. But I'd say that any of these are suitable for a princess. In fact, if you don't mind, I may use some for my other rich clients. The few who are left."

"But I want my entry to be special," Phoenix said. "It has to be the best. Otherwise, I won't win the contest. I'd better keep on drawing. May I have more paper, please?"

"No," the shoemaker said. "If you want to make more sketches, you'll have to use the backs of these papers."

"But—"

"No buts!" And Percy Snailkips walked away.

Whelk was staring at her. "How did you do so much in one afternoon?"

"I'm in one of my moods. One of my grand, flighty moods, Aunt Twisle would say."

"You almost seem like you're—well, enchanted."

Phoenix laughed loudly. "You and your magic. Who'd want to cast a spell on me? No, I've just got to win the contest, that's all. I've got to. Which sketch do you like best?"

Whelk paced in front of the sketches on the wall, one hand stroking the carving hanging from a thong around his neck.

"I think they're all good," he said. "But, listen, are you thinking too much about the shoes and not enough about the princesses?"

"What do you mean?"

"Well, you've met them both. What would they like? Which shoes would they crave and why? Think about that. Then you'll know which sketch to pick."

After Whelk left, Phoenix took her least favorite sketch off the wall, turned it over, and sat at her bench with her eyes closed. As picture after picture of shoes flashed in her mind, she had to sit on her hands to keep from drawing. Slow down, she told herself. Breathe. Think of Princess Batissa. Rora's face behind bars popped into her mind, but she pushed it out.

"Think of Princess Batissa," Phoenix whispered.

She pictured the princess in her yellow dress. The princess hated yellow—that was a clue. Perhaps she would like a pair of shoes with every color of the rainbow except yellow. No, not shoes, ankle-high boots—to show as much color as possible. And around the top edges, ruffles of white feathers would set off the colors. Phoenix drew the design. Perfect. And not expensive either.

Phoenix took another sketch off the wall and turned it over. She closed her eyes, picturing Princess Aurantica, who would be queen someday. Her shoes should show the weight of that honor. Maybe a scene from Windward's history? But what did Princess Aurantica want? Phoenix remembered how the princess had stood with her hand on the leopard, looking out the window. How stiff she had been, how unhappy she had seemed. Maybe what Aurantica wanted more than anything else was a moment of freedom from her responsibilities, a moment of escape.

But how could Phoenix express that in a pair of shoes? Princess Aurantica had been looking out at the sea, a place where the spirit could soar. Could Phoenix make a pair of shoes that looked like the sea? They would show freedom and yet would still be an appropriate symbol of the archipelago kingdom that Princess Aurantica would rule one day. Phoenix would marble a piece of white silk with waves of blue. Yes! And to fasten the latchets, white scallop shells. Very simple and pure—and again, inexpensive.

Phoenix drew a sketch, and although it looked fine, she was still uncertain. After she pinned the rainbow boots and the high-heeled sea slippers on the wall, she took down ten more sketches and began to crowd more shoe drawings onto the back of each one. Five minutes passed, ten minutes, then an hour, then two hours. She did not eat. She did not drink. She did not stop to go to the water closet even though she needed to. Her hand could not stop drawing. The tight knot of pain in her chest spread across her body until it seemed as if a wolf were howling inside her.

Phoenix scratched her face with her blackened hands and began to cry in frustration. None of the sketches were good enough. All of them were horrible, terrible. Something was wrong with them, just as something was wrong with the princesses. She would never win the contest, never be Shoemaker to the Royal Household. Phoenix kept drawing and drawing and drawing, still burning inside, but now blistering, scorched. Where was the perfect sketch? She had so many ideas, why couldn't she find the right one, the perfect one?

Whelk came up to her and gently pried the charcoal out of her hand.

"You must stop, Phoenix," he said. "I think you're ill. Why are you so driven?"

"I don't know!" she cried. "I can't stop drawing. I can't ever stop! Why? Why? Why can't I stop!" And she put her head down on her bench and began to sob.

8

The Magic Cloak

BENEATH A SKY AS BLUE AS ONE OF Nemaree's priestess's veils, Whelk walked Phoenix home from the shop. She sobbed and talked all the way.

"I can't go home," she cried, "I can't. I have to make the princesses' shoes. They don't have faces. They must at least have shoes."

"You'll make their shoes all right," Whelk said, "but not today. Listen, you heard the master; he promised to save all your sketches. And the shoes don't have to be submitted for almost two more weeks. You've got to get well first. Something's wrong with you, Phoenix. You're as wound up as a spring."

"You just want me to go home so you can use my designs and enter the contest yourself!"

Whelk stopped. "What a rotten thing to say."

"It's true. I know it's true! Or maybe the master is going to use them to get his royal appointment back. He's going to steal my ideas!"

"Now I know you're sick. Otherwise, you'd never accuse your friends like this. What's the matter with you? Where are you, Phoenix? You seem like you're in some other world."

Phoenix rubbed her forehead. "I'm sorry. It's Rora. I'm just worried about Rora. Let's go to the prison and visit her, please!"

"No. Listen, the master said to take you straight home. Straight home. You're sick, Phoenix. Don't you understand?"

As they turned on to her beloved Harbor Road, with all its bustle, its shouting vendors and entertainers, its shops, sights, and smells, Phoenix stopped dead.

"No," she said, backing away. "I can't bear it. There's too much going on. Let's take the alley instead." But even in the alley the world assaulted her wherever she looked. An orange door made her shudder with its brightness. Phoenix averted her eyes, only to see a ragged patch of green grass growing against a red-brick wall. The colors were too vivid, the contrast too sharp. She tried looking up, but the line of buildings against the sky made a blue chute, and her thoughts went zooming down it.

In the next block of the alley, flapping amid the lines of washing hanging between the second stories, a yellow tablecloth glowed like a rectangular sun. Phoenix clutched Whelk's arm and looked away, focusing on the dirt a few steps ahead of her feet. That, however, did not keep her from hearing a woman singing as she swept her back steps. She sang "The Siren on the Rock," about a man who crashed his ship on the Siren Rock as the siren lured him with her wild song. The woman's voice was beautiful, piercing, and too sweet to bear, the story too sad for Phoenix's sore heart.

Phoenix clapped her hands over her ears and moaned. "Make her stop, make him stop! Don't let him crash, don't let him drown!"

All her defenses had been swept away. Phoenix felt as though she had no filters to catch what came at her from the world—things that she saw, things that people said or did—so all these things slammed straight into the core of her, straight into the whirling mix of emotions and thoughts and stirred them up more. She was a whirlpool, a cyclone, a mess.

They hurried away from the singing. When the sound had faded into the background, Whelk took off the cord hanging around his neck.

"Do you know who this is?" He nodded toward the carved figure dangling on the end of the cord. It looked like a winged dolphin.

"It's Ethalass," Phoenix said. "The sea god who rescues the drowning."

"I think you're drowning now, so I want you to have it."
And Whelk put the cord over her head.

Phoenix clasped the carving. "I'm drowning in air. I'm
skimming like a flying fish on top of the sea. But a fish can't
breathe air. I can't seem to breathe. My chest burns." Then
Phoenix remembered what the tall boy standing beside the
burn barrel had said: "Too much fire can kill."

At home, her aunts took one look at her and sent for
Healer Torris. He had treated Phoenix once before when
one of her flighty moods possessed her. He gave her a sleeping draft and waited for it to take effect. It did not. He gave
her a second, stronger dose, and then, finally, Phoenix did
sleep. When she woke, her chest felt raw and sore.

"There you are, awake at last," said Aunt Twisle, sitting
down in the chintz chair with a pile of printed pamphlets
in one hand. She had stayed home to take care of Phoenix.
"I practiced my entire part for *The Princess and the Dragon*
and you didn't stir a bit. Not even during the jetés."

"How long did I sleep?"

"About sixteen hours. How are you feeling?"

"Tired," Phoenix said. "And achy. But the bees are less
buzzy."

Aunt Twisle put the pamphlets on the low table in front
of the sofa and began folding them in half one by one.
Phoenix read the words "Join the Archipelago Party" in big
letters on the top line.

"I wish we knew why you have these flighty moods," she
said. "Healer Torris says you're very sensitive and get wound

up easily. But it seems to me it's more than that. He says we need to keep you very quiet for a few days."

"But I have to make the shoes for the contest and go to see—"

"You will. Liona talked to Percy Snailkips. You may go back to the shop as soon as you're rested and calm—and I mean calm. I want you to stay home for at least three days and do nothing but rest. You'll still have ten days to make the shoes. Everyone at the shop will help you when you go back. Understand?"

Phoenix nodded.

"The sooner you're better, the sooner you can go back to the shop. So part of that depends on how much you co-operate."

Phoenix pulled up the quilt and sighed. "But I want to visit Rora."

"You couldn't even if you were well enough. They don't allow children who aren't relatives to visit the prisoners."

"What's going to happen to her?"

"She'll plead guilty to the charge of destroying public property, not guilty to sedition. Her trial is in two weeks. My guess is they will drop the charge of sedition and give her a taste of a few months in prison. It may be just what she needs to curb her impatience. If they do find her guilty of sedition, it could be a sentence of several years."

"Years?" Phoenix whispered, tasting bile in her mouth.

"Yes. What she did was very foolish." Aunt Twisle ran her thumb along a fold, creasing it.

"Rora said the adults in the Archipelago Party never change anything. She wanted to do something. To act."

"There are many ways to bring about change," Aunt Twisle said. "Violence and destruction are one way. I prefer to work peacefully. I think that brings about more effective change. But things are never fast enough for the young. Folding and passing out pamphlets isn't very glamorous." She sighed. "A revolution is coming."

"When?" asked Phoenix.

"Perhaps next year. Either the queen and the great lords and ladies in the House of Islands will have to accept a second House of Parliament or things will get ugly. Now remember, you must never tell anyone you were at the Parliament Building that night."

"What if Rora tells?"

"She won't. It will be a matter of pride with her to keep it secret." Aunt Twisle finished folding the stack of pamphlets. "There, all ready for tomorrow. Enough talking now. You need rest. The healer left more sleeping medicine in case you can't sleep tonight. He said we must get you sleeping all night again. If you don't get better soon, I really think we should take you to see a mederi up on Healer's Hill."

Phoenix agreed. The mederi were great healers who had trained in the famous school and hospital up on Healer's Hill, a bluff to the south of the city. They had more knowledge than healers like Torris. Some people said they used magic arts in their healing practice.

"How would you like to hem a blanket for Rora to use in prison?" Aunt Twisle asked. "I've got that big old piece of heavy blue wool that I've been wondering what to do with. Hemming it will keep you quiet and yet you'll feel like you're doing something for Rora."

"All right."

"I'll get it out right after I make you some lunch." And Aunt Twisle went into the kitchen.

Phoenix curled up on the sofa and with her forefinger traced the black and white diamonds on the red quilt. When Aunt Twisle banged some pots in the kitchen, Phoenix winced; the noise was too loud. The light filtering through the lace curtains on the window was too bright. The skulls behind the curving glass doors on the curio cabinet were too hard and sharp. She burrowed under the quilt and pulled a pillow over her head. Her whole body seemed to be one raw, exposed nerve. Phoenix wanted quiet, blackness—no movement. She had to protect her senses from everything. A few days ago, she had run through the market craving stimulation, reveling in cherry blossoms, blasts of wind, and bright red ribbons. She shuddered to think of it. Now she wanted none of that fiery delight; it brought her too much pain. How had it all changed so fast? At what moment had it all become too much? It was as though she had entered a different room inside herself.

Two long days passed. Slowly, the pain in Phoenix's chest changed from a stabbing sharpness to a dull, heavy ache.

She slept each night all night, thanks to the sleeping medicine. During the day, she sat on the sofa pushing the needle in and out on Rora's blanket, her thoughts blank, her hands clumsy and slow.

On the third day, back at the shop at last, Phoenix stared at the sketches on the wall, amazed by what she had done in her frenzy. She could not imagine doing it now. She could hardly imagine drawing one sketch. The charcoal seemed as though it would be too heavy to lift. She took down the sketches of the rainbow boot and the sea slippers.

"Welcome back." Percy Snailkips stood beside her, his hands clasped over his stomach. "We missed you."

"These two," Phoenix said.

He nodded. "Simple, but elegant. And inexpensive. A wise choice. Here are the lasts of the princesses' feet."

Phoenix took one of the lasts and ran her fingers over it, feeling the smooth, well-oiled wood. Suddenly the task ahead seemed huge. Where would she find the strength? She felt so tired, as worn out as the worn-out shoes.

Ten days later, with Whelk's and the shoemaker's help, Phoenix finished making both pairs of shoes. Her hands were stained with blue dye from marbling the white silk for the sea slippers, and her fingertips were sore from sewing all the white feathers onto the rainbow boots. She wrote her name in pencil on the linings of the shoes, then wrapped them in muslin, packed them in boxes, and delivered them to the Master of the Royal Wardrobe at the palace. Although the shoes had turned out as lovely as her sketches, Phoenix found she was too tired to care whether she won or lost the contest.

On her way home from the palace, she decided to walk past Five Towers Prison, even though it was out of her way. Her feet did not seem to be working right. She had to concentrate on picking up each foot and setting it down in front of her. Why did walking take so much effort? Why did everything take so much effort? When Phoenix at last reached the prison she stood outside, looking up.

The five towers clustered together like the five clenched fingers of a fist. A light, drizzling rain fell, turning the stone a dark, sleek gray. Only a few barred windows broke the forbidding façade, but she waved anyway on the off chance that Rora might be looking out. Phoenix could not bear to think of Rora locked up in there.

Phoenix knew that if she had not run away from the Parliament Building that night, she would be locked up in those cold stone towers, too. Part of her felt she should not have left Rora, left her to suffer in prison all alone. And yet, another part of Phoenix was relieved that she was free. Phoenix ran her tongue over the roof of her mouth, drew a long sharp breath, then turned away and plodded toward home.

She had just reached Anemone Street when she saw a man carrying a bag of grain accidentally knock over an old woman. He did not stop to help her up.

"Scoundrel!" The old woman shook her fist at him. "Have

you no heart for a poor foreign woman, a stranger in this city? I say fie on Faranor! Fie, if all its citizens are like you!"

"No, old mother," Phoenix said to her. "Don't judge us all by him. Let me help you up." The old woman's face was like a dried fig, brown and wrinkled, but her blue eyes were bright.

"Have you any chocolate?" she asked as Phoenix helped her stand. Phoenix collected the woman's oak stick and her burlap sack, which she had dropped.

"No, no chocolate," Phoenix said. "But there, you're all right now."

The old woman leaned against the seawall, breathing heavily, while the waves pounded below. She wore a blue jacket with fur trim and a full, brown, pleated skirt that had a dark stain from her fall on the wet cobblestones.

"Where are you from?" Phoenix asked.

"Honorath."

Phoenix stepped back. Honorath, home of the famous wizards' school, was in the eastern part of the Eastern Reach, where the lands were said to be thick with magic.

"Not so brave as you seem at first, eh, girl?" The old woman laughed. She still had most of her teeth, but they were as brown as walnuts. She hoisted her bag and began to limp along, leaning heavily on the oak stick. Phoenix looked at the old woman's bare feet, which were rough and red and covered with chilblains.

"May I carry your bag to your lodging?" Phoenix asked, tired though she was.

"Very well, but I have no lodging yet, dearie. I just walked off the worthy ship the *Mysterious Lady*, and the land rolls under my poor sore feet. In two days I set sail for Idyllwyld in the Southern Reach."

Phoenix thought fast. The old woman did not look as though she had much money.

"You might try the Three Maids Inn," Phoenix suggested. "Or the Misty Reach. Don't go to the Lookout, though. They've got fleas in the beds."

"What's your name, dearie?" the old woman asked, handing over her sack.

"Phoenix."

"Phoenix! That's a grand name for a wisp of a miss with blue hands. A great bird rising from the bitterness of ash to the glory of flame and then to ash again. Flame to ash, ash to flame in an endless cycle over and over days without end. Is such your fate? You look as gray as ash just now. Tired as an old woman yourself." She limped along, wincing with each step.

"Wait a minute." Phoenix stopped, unlaced her right shoe, and pulled it off. "Here, try this on. It might fit you."

"Well, a sweetie dear you are," the old woman said, "even if you don't have any chocolate for me." And she pulled on the shoe. "It fits, with a little room to spare in the toe. That's good. Never know when a little hiding place might come in handy." She winked.

Phoenix took off her left shoe and gave it to the old woman, who slipped it on the other foot.

"There, now in a few weeks, your feet will heal," Phoenix said as she pulled off her brown socks. She gave those to the woman, too, then wiggled her toes on the wet cobblestones and tried not to think of what the shoemaker would say about the shoes or what Aunt Mulgaussy would say about the socks.

After the old woman took off the shoes, pulled on the socks, and put the shoes back on again—puffing a little with the effort of bending over—Phoenix saw her safely to the Misty Reach.

"One good turn deserves another," the old woman said at the door. She untied her burlap sack and pulled out a plain cloak, the fine silvery wool darned in places. "This cloak comes from the island of Drulane in the Eastern Reach," she explained. "The women weavers there are all wizards, every one. As you can see, sweetie dear, it is very old. I know it doesn't look like much, but it has great power. It will keep you hidden well."

"Keep me hidden?"

The old woman held up one gnarled finger, stained green. "It is a cloak of invisibility and illusion. When you wear it, two things will happen. First, when others look upon you, you will be invisible to their eyes. Just let them try to see you, just let them try! A better chance they'll have of seeing the moon turn somersaults." She laughed.

"And the second thing?" Phoenix asked, breathless.

"When you wear the cloak and look out upon the world,

you will see through all spells of illusion." She tapped Phoenix's nose. "Be sure to darn any holes right away. Common thread will do. Use it well, sweetie dear. May it bring you luck. I think you need some." And with that, the old woman picked up her sack and hobbled into the inn.

9

In the Nethersea

WHEN PHOENIX REACHED HOME with the gray cloak bundled beneath her arm, no one was there. She stood in the middle of the parlor, shook out the cloak, and watched the ripples of cloth unfold smoothly, silently; not one wrinkle showed in the fine wool. Phoenix threw the cloak around her shoulders and looked down at herself. Nothing happened. She did not disappear. Had the old woman from Honorath been telling tales?

The silver clasp at the throat tapered like a tongue of flame. Phoenix fastened it, then looked down at her feet; they had vanished. She cried out. Her legs and the rest of her body had vanished, too. Her hands, which she could not see, rubbed the fine wool of the cloak, which she could not see either. She could smell it, though, smell burlap, daisies, and chocolate.

When she looked in the mirror in her aunts' bedchamber, Phoenix saw only her head, floating, because she had not pulled up the cloak's hood. Her face looked pale, her brown eyes huge. Her hair, pulled back in a braid—ending abruptly where it fell beneath the cloak—appeared redder than usual. She was afraid she might vanish forever if she pulled up the hood, and too much of her was lost already. As Phoenix stood there staring, she felt a pressure in the back of her throat, in the back of her eyes, and she began to cry.

"Nothing," she whispered. "It's all nothing." Her tears dripped off her chin, shining droplets falling through the air. She swallowed hard and unfastened the silver clasp. When her body reappeared, she patted her arms and legs to reassure herself of her reality.

Phoenix took off the cloak, began to fold it up, then stopped. Why not use the cloak to free Rora from prison? Phoenix could sneak in, find Rora, throw the cloak around her, and sneak her out. Then Phoenix sighed, wiping her eyes, seeing the difficulties with the scheme. Even a magic cloak could not get her through stone and locked doors. And besides, she was so tired . . . No, she would wait until after the trial and see how much prison time the Giver of Justice gave Rora. If it was years, then yes, Phoenix would try to help her escape. She finished folding the cloak.

If her aunts found out about the cloak, Phoenix knew they would take it away, fearing the magic. She would like to show it to Whelk. Maybe she could sneak it to work somehow and show it to him in secret, though how that would be possible in the busy shop she did not know. Meanwhile, Phoenix hid the cloak in the bottom of her cedar chest, which she had inherited from her mother. In it, she kept all her special things—two of her mother's baby dresses that Phoenix, too, had worn, a pair of her mother's dancing slippers, a white shirt of her father's, a ten-inch square of gold brocade she had found behind a dress shop, and a small silver ring she had worn as a baby. It would not even fit on her pinkie finger now.

After she closed the cedar chest, Phoenix was too exhausted to do anything except go to bed. She could not bear to hear one more noise, one more word. She could not bear to lift her head, or to speak. If only she could hide inside a dark, quiet hole in the bottom of the sea where no one could find her. Phoenix pulled out her quilts from the closet, wrapped them around herself, and then collapsed onto the sofa. Though she was still awake when her aunts came home an hour later, she pretended to be asleep.

"Well, here she is, sleeping almost as sweetly as she might in Trebonness," Aunt Mulgaussy said. "Bless her."

"Let her sleep, poor darling," Aunt Twisle whispered. They went into their bedchamber, and the door clicked behind them.

They woke Phoenix for supper.

"I'm not hungry," she said.

"Not hungry!" Aunt Liona exclaimed. "But it's sausages

—the cheese-filled ones. A treat, and your favorite. Hungry now?"

Phoenix shook her head. Aunt Twisle put her hand on Phoenix's forehead.

"No fever," Aunt Twisle said.

"I'm just tired." Phoenix began to cry. "The shoes I made were no good at all. Nothing is any good. There's no reason . . . to do anything." She sobbed. "It's all useless. Why did I bother to enter the contest? I'll never amount to anything. It's all nothing. Nothing." Her chest ached again, but instead of a sharp pain, it was a dull crushing ache that seemed to drag her downward, pulverizing her beneath its weight. She touched Ethalass, still hanging around her neck, but the god did not help her. She was drowning.

All three aunts looked at each other.

"The Nethersea," they said together and then sighed. Phoenix had been in the Nethersea several times before, usually right after she had been in one of her frenzied, flighty moods. It was a dark, sad, terrible place that she did not have the strength to hate.

She sobbed harder and pulled the quilt over her head.

"We have good news for you, Phoenix," Aunt Twisle said when she and Aunt Liona came home on Moonday afternoon. Phoenix lay on the sofa, as she had for the past two days.

"Spectacular news!" Aunt Liona cried.

"Let me guess," said Aunt Mulgaussy, who had stayed home with Phoenix. "Ebbon Lloyd wants to marry me!"

"Better yet," Aunt Twisle said. "Rora's trial is over. She was found guilty of destroying public property but innocent of sedition. Thank the Sea Maid! The Giver of Justice gave her a one-month sentence and a fine of ten gold pieces. Since Rora's family couldn't pay the fine, the judge increased the sentence to twelve weeks, including the time she's already spent there."

"All in all, it isn't as bad as it might have been," Aunt Liona said. "The Giver of Justice, she went easy on Rora because of her youth. I think we should celebrate."

"Celebrate?" Phoenix saw Rora's face pressed up against bars, saw Rora alone, trapped and crying. Phoenix fought back her own tears. "Did you see her? How did she look?"

"Fine," Aunt Twisle said. "A bit subdued for Rora, but fine."

Phoenix sat up. "Did she send any message for me?"

"We didn't get a chance to talk to her," Aunt Liona said.

Phoenix slumped back on the sofa. "She hasn't answered the letter I sent with the blanket."

"I'm sure she will," Aunt Twisle said, "now that the trial is over. But I'm worried about you. You've been inside for three days now. Why not go out and get some fresh air?"

"I don't feel like going anywhere. I'm too tired."

"Nonsense," Aunt Mulgaussy said. "A walk would cheer you up and help bring you out of the Nethersea. The great-granddaughter of Seagraine Dance does not mope. Make an effort, Phoenix. Cheer up."

"Don't you think I'd cheer up if I could!" Phoenix shouted. "Stop saying that. It doesn't help!"

Aunt Mulgaussy pursed her lips and went into the bed-chamber.

Finally, because Phoenix could not stand the worried looks on her aunts' faces, she dragged herself off the sofa and went out into the city. Usually when she wanted to distract herself, Phoenix went to Harbor Road, where there was always something to watch—jugglers or singers or dancers—that could take her mind off her troubles. But she was still feeling too raw and fragile for all that bustle, so instead she walked north along Majesty Bay. She thought of walking to Five Towers Prison but knew she would burst into tears the moment she saw it.

It was an ugly day. Gray clouds wrinkled over the water like a great rumpled brow. The frigates, schooners, and pinnaces sailing in the bay skimmed along, departing or arriving with their sails unfurled. On Phoenix's right, the gray surf pounded the stones of the seawall. She stared down at the frothing swirls. Why not throw herself in the water and let the tide take her far out to sea? She would float, her hair would float around her face until she sank and died. The Black Ship would come for her soul and take it away the Goddess knew where. But when Phoenix imagined how cold the water would be, she shivered and looked away.

After she had plodded along for fifteen minutes, her feet pinched and cold in her old holey shoes because she had given her new shoes to the old woman—how Aunt Mulgaussy had scolded when she found out!—Phoenix came to the shipyards where the best ships in Windward were built. Men walked along the wharves carrying coils of rope and rolls of sailcloth on their shoulders. Two men passed her, each carrying one end of a long two-handed saw, which wobbled and sang *wha wha wha*, flashing silver. Phoenix smelled tar, sawdust, and sweat. Shouting and the sound of hammering rang through the air. Phoenix winced; it was all too loud for her raw nerves. She was about to turn away when she saw a crowd gathered on the third pier. Standing in front was a royal carriage, painted blue and gilded gold, drawn by four white horses with golden plumes on their heads. Phoenix walked closer.

A new ship was moored beside the pier, a six-masted schooner flying the flags of Windward and the Royal Navy. Sailors in blue uniforms stood at attention on the deck. Then Phoenix saw the name, *Aurantica*, painted in white letters on the hull, and she understood why the royal carriage was there.

High in the bow, standing alone near the carved figurehead of a woman, was Princess Aurantica. She wore a gray wool cape with a hood lined with gray fur hanging down. A circlet of silver crowned her head. Her light brown hair, long and loose, blew over her face. She was not smiling. She held a bouquet of white lilies a little away from her body, as though she did not want them to touch her. Phoenix, elbowing her way to the front of the crowd, saw grief in the curve of Aurantica's neck, grief in the drooping lilies, grief in the prow of the ship.

A wizard with a long black beard stood beside her. Phoenix recognized Fengal, Whelk's uncle, whom Percy Snailkips had pointed out to her in the palace. He raised his staff in the air and spoke.

"Let this new ship go forward to fight the Order of the Black Dragon. They seek to raise their own navy to sail against us, seizing merchant ships in the Belica Straits. But so long as we have brave ships and brave sailors and bright spells to fight against them, I say, we shall prevail." Everyone cheered. Then the wizard turned to the princess. "If you would like to dedicate the ship now, Your Highness?"

"I dedicate this ship, the *Aurantica*," the princess said, "in the name of Nemaree, Great Mother of all. May this ship always sail with a true wind. May she battle bravely for Windward. And . . . and may she have the power to go wherever her heart guides her." Princess Aurantica raised her arms toward the wooden figurehead, carved with a likeness of her own face frozen in a grimacing smile. When she flung the lilies, they arched up, struck the figurehead, and then scattered as they fell into the water below. The princess stood stiffly for a moment, her arms still raised.

Phoenix watched the flowers sink into the water one at a time until they vanished. Then, strangely, as she closed her eyes, Phoenix seemed to see the bruised lilies above her because she was in the water, too, down deep in the Nethersea; and if she held up her hands, she could catch the lilies because they were floating downward into her open palms.

As the crowd cheered, Princess Aurantica walked down the gangway onto the pier. Then the crowd began to thin. The sailors scurried over the decks and pier, untying ropes, making ready to sail. The princess seemed alone though she stood beside the wizard and the captain in his tricorn hat. Phoenix inched closer, wanting the princess to recognize her. They shared something—grief, a heaviness of heart. It would be a relief to speak to someone who understood.

"Take me with you," Princess Aurantica said to the captain.

"Your Highness?" the captain asked, startled.

"Take me to the land of the dragons, where the flame burns brightly."

"You speak in riddles, Princess," said the captain.

"Are you unwell?" asked Fengal. "Allow me to summon one of your ladies."

He called to the two ladies-in-waiting hovering nearby. "The princess is unwell, take her back to her carriage."

"No," Princess Aurantica said. "Let me sail to the land of the dragons—see them dance, see them fly, see them burn."

"Come, Your Highness." A lady-in-waiting put one hand on the princess's arm and led her back to the carriage. A moment later, it rolled away, the horses' gilded hooves flashing, their golden plumes waving.

Phoenix walked back along Majesty Bay until, too tired

to take another step, she sat down on the edge of the seawall and panted as though she had been running instead of creeping along the road. She thought about the sea slippers she had made for Princess Aurantica, wondered if the princess had seen them yet, then found she did not even care.

"Nothing," she whispered. "Just nothing."

After resting, Phoenix walked twenty more steps before she stopped again. Sick with pain and exhaustion, she leaned against the seawall and watched the water swirl below, gray and beckoning, speckled with white spume, deep. She kept swallowing and swallowing; there seemed to be a hole in her throat, and her self was running out of it. She walked home, raw and cold, taking one slow step after another, as though she were walking on the bottom of the black sea with bruised lilies floating around her.

10

Mederi Gale

FOR THE NEXT THREE DAYS, PHOENIX STAYED on the sofa in the parlor. The purple walls, which she had always found so gay, seemed somber now, and they filled her with a vague dread, especially the corners of the room where the shadows gathered in clots. On the top shelf of the curio cabinet lay the skulls of the lemur and parrot; the clean, white bones had always impressed her with their delicacy and beauty. Now, however, the skulls seemed to leer at her, to chatter unspeakable horrors that she could not quite catch. Phoenix was afraid that in her despair she, too, was becoming a curiosity, a freak, a horror.

"Please, please take the skulls away," she begged Aunt Liona, who was staying home with her that day. Aunt Liona put them in a sack and then opened the front door.

"Where are you going?" Phoenix rose halfway off the sofa.

"Just to the cellar, to put these in our storage room," Aunt Liona said.

"No! Don't go. I don't want to be alone, please. Don't leave me here alone!"

"All right. Don't get upset. I'll put them in the bedchamber."

Phoenix lay back on the sofa. She was afraid that her aunts would vanish, afraid that now she was sick they would not want her anymore. Everything seemed to be slipping away from her. She felt as fragile as a web, as though all the parts of herself were linked by delicate filaments of shining thread. The least wind, a harsh word, or the slightest touch by an outside hand would break the filament, and she would unravel, broken. Her hand went to Ethalass. The carving of the winged dolphin was hanging on the brown cord around her neck, but she was drowning in spite of it.

As the days passed, she ate toast and a little pea soup but nothing else because food had no taste. At night, Phoenix slept only one or two hours in spite of the sleeping medicine. It wasn't working any longer. "What is the answer?" she whispered again and again into the darkness, but she was too exhausted to form the question. In the moonlight, the costume rack, heaped with clothes, wigs, and hats, looked like a shaggy shuffling monster.

As she lay looking at it, Phoenix felt great fear, but she

could not say what she feared, only that her hands felt afraid, her legs felt afraid, her knees, elbows, face, and back felt afraid. The fear tasted like tin. She hurt all over, and she was certain she had caught some terrible disease that would surely kill her. Her body seemed to have turned into a red-hot sore. A horrible finger with a crusty black nail kept digging and scratching the sore over and over again.

"Let me go," she whispered. It was as though she wrestled with some loathsome thing dredged up from the deep places inside her. It had arms and legs that pummeled her, teeth that sank into her until she bled. It was her despair, her grief, everything she feared and hated, and it tried to drag her under.

When Phoenix had been in the Nethersea before, the black mood had lasted for days, sometimes weeks. Now she began to fear it would never end, and her eyes traced the marigold trim between the ceiling and the walls around and around in endless, hopeless circles. On the fifth day, she looked at the curio cabinet and saw her own skull sitting on the shelf, gleaming, white, mocking her. It was her skull, her face, but without a face—like the statue of the princesses. Phoenix closed her eyes, but she still saw it, still heard it gibbering like some kind of demon. Then, late that night, she saw it breathing, and its breath was a snaking flame that flickered out from the mouth, then slithered in, out, then in, over and over again, making the bony white teeth glow red-orange. She cried then, and the sound was a wilderness of grief howling from deep inside her stomach, the braying of an animal in pain. It woke her aunts, who came and threw their arms around her while she sobbed.

On the afternoon of the seventh day, Percy Snailkips came to visit.

"Phoenix Dance," he said. "Get up. Be sad no more!"

"What is it?" she asked. Her voice sounded low and gravelly, ancient and worn.

"You must get up and come back to the shop. We need you. You have shoes to make. I bear good tidings. You won the contest!"

Phoenix stared at him. "I what?" She had heard him, but she wanted him to say it again, because she had felt nothing move inside her when he spoke, no joy, no hope.

"You won the contest! You've received an appointment as Shoemaker to the Royal Household! You've done it, Phoenix. Kloud's Bounty! You've brought dignity and trade back to the shop. Just as you said you would."

"It's a mistake," she said. "Besides, I'm too tired to make anything. I'm sure it's all a mistake."

"No mistake," the shoemaker said. "See? I brought the letter from the Master of the Royal Wardrobe." And he put the parchment in her hands.

As she held it, Phoenix began to cry because she felt no happiness at all. She felt as if she had wrapped herself in the magic cloak, and her self had vanished. It was as though her thoughts had shattered into a thousand pieces, and the pieces had been put back together wrong. She could not figure out the puzzle.

"I need to take a bath," Phoenix said. "If I could only take a bath, I'm sure I would have the answer to all of this."

"Don't you understand, Phoenix?" Aunt Twisle said. "Your dream has come true!"

"But there's a cold wind blowing across the bones!" Phoenix cried. "I'm afraid! It's coming from my skull in the curio cabinet. Cover it up! Why doesn't someone cover it up? And put out the fire—its breath is burning! Oh, I hurt. I want to die!"

It was then, she learned later, that her aunts went to Healer's Hill to find a mederi.

Phoenix lay huddled and wretched beneath her quilt on the sofa listening to Mederi Cerinthe Gale, whose voice seemed to drift across a cold, dark sea.

"Phoenix," the mederi said, "I suspect you have the Illness of the Two Kingdoms: the Kingdom of Brilliance and the Kingdom of Darkness."

"But I've never lived anywhere . . . in any kingdom but Windward." Each word dropped like a stone from Phoenix's lips.

"The name of the illness refers to a state of mind, not to a real place," the mederi said. "The illness makes you swing from brilliance to darkness, and back again."

Phoenix could not find the will to lift her tongue. The red quilt with its black and white diamonds seemed to be made of lead, crushing her bones. Her chest was a cave of pain. With an effort, she slid her eyes to the back of the parlor, where her three aunts hovered in front of the purple walls.

Mederi Gale took Phoenix's hand. The sleeve of the mederi's white muslin robe, which seemed dazzlingly bright, brushed Phoenix's wrist.

"Let me explain," the mederi said. "You spend your life traveling between these two kingdoms in your mind. In the Kingdom of Brilliance your mood is elated. You're bursting with ideas and vigor—at first. But soon your thoughts come so fast that they grow muddled. You rush from one thing to another, and you talk too much. Then your nerves and your senses are so aroused that everything brings great pain. Then you slide into an episode of the Kingdom of Darkness, or the Nethersea, where your mood becomes despairing. You feel sadness, blackness, stillness. More pain. Where you are now."

Where she was now. Phoenix plucked at a seam in the blue sofa that had split open; raw stuffing oozed from the hole.

"Sometimes you are well for a while," the mederi added, "but sooner or later you soar into the Kingdom of Brilliance or sink into the Kingdom of Darkness. And then, as sure as the sun sets, the other follows. The cycle repeats over and over."

"Yes," Phoenix whispered, her throat dry, staring at the empty yellow cup on the table beside the sofa. She sank onto her pillow. Her hair, unwashed for days, dragged down-ward from her scalp.

"I'm so tired," she whispered.

Mederi Gale leaned closer. "Perhaps I can help you." Her hand, large and warm and strong, pressed Phoenix's hand. "Your aunts have told me about your childhood. Now I want you to tell me about the past few months."

For the next two hours Mederi Gale held Phoenix's hand, listening to the tale of her life since the day she had seen the sign *Apprentice wanted, inquire within*, until the moment she had learned she had won the contest. Phoenix told her everything, even what had happened at the Parliament Building, about everything, that is, except the magic cloak. In her exhaustion, Phoenix often grew confused in the tell-ing, and her aunts chimed in to set things straight.

"A fascinating story," the mederi said when Phoenix had finished. By now it was late afternoon, and the light slanting through the window fell in a block across the pine floor, burnishing it gold. "I'll need to do a complete physical ex-amination, but I believe your story confirms my diagnosis. You do have the Illness of the Two Kingdoms, an emotional illness. A serious, though not dangerous, case."

"Not dangerous!" Aunt Liona exclaimed. "Look at her!"

"Yes, she is ill," said Mederi Gale. "But when people with dangerous cases are in the Kingdom of Brilliance, they put their lives at risk by thinking they can fly or something of that nature. Or they think they are gods. In short, they be-come mad. Many end up in asylums."

Asylums. Phoenix shivered.

"And," the mederi added, "those critically ill in the Kingdom of Darkness feel so much pain and sorrow that they try to end their lives. It can be a very dangerous illness."

A strand of dark blond hair had slipped from the braid the mederi wore coiled at the nape of her neck. When she pushed the strand behind her ear, the silver dewdrop earrings she wore swayed, catching the light. Phoenix stared at them, wishing she could hold some of that light inside her self.

"I'm not sure I understand this," Aunt Twisle said. "Aren't we all happy sometimes and sad other times? Don't we all have swings in our moods?"

"Of course," said Mederi Gale. "But people with this illness swing much further back and forth than the rest of us."

Phoenix had an image of herself swinging on a swing. As she soared up into the air with her legs stuck straight out in front of her, she swung into the Kingdom of Brilliance; then, with a swooping rush toward the ground and up again on the other side, she swung backward into the Kingdom of Darkness.

"Can't she cheer up if she just makes an effort?" Aunt Mulgaussy asked.

Phoenix felt an explosion of anger in her chest.

"No," Mederi Gale said. "No more than you could wish yourself well if you had a fever."

"What causes this illness?" Aunt Twisle asked.

"I don't know," the mederi said.

"What is the cure?" Aunt Liona asked.

"Yes," Phoenix said, "a cure."

"I'm afraid there is no cure," Mederi Gale said. "But I've been experimenting with different treatments. For you I think I might try bloodletting. The Kingdom of Darkness may be triggered by an excess of black bile. Bloodletting may help change that balance."

"Will it hurt?" Phoenix asked.

"A little. I see you're wearing Ethalass, who helps the drowning. You might also pray to the Sea Maid, who helps those lost at sea and those lost in their hearts, which I think you are right now."

Phoenix nodded, her fingers still pulling at the stuffing. She looked at the curio cabinet. She could still see her skull sitting there. "Am I . . . am I a freak?" she asked the mederi.

"No. You are ill. A sick person is not a freak. At the moment, I'm working with three other people who have this illness. I must be honest, though. This illness is a great challenge. I still have a lot to learn about it. It's tricky, very tricky!" She sighed. "My treatments haven't been completely successful yet. But if we approach the problem logically, and experiment again and again, I'm certain that one day we will find an effective way to treat the illness. If you will trust me, I'll do the best I can for you. My goal is to find some way to cut off your high and low moods, so you can lead an almost normal life."

Phoenix stopped plucking at the stuffing. If she could lead a normal life, if she was not sick and moody and hideous, then her aunts would still want her.

"Now I'd like to begin the physical examination," the mederi said. "And then I will bleed you."

11

Bitter Herbs

THAT NIGHT PHOENIX LAY ON THE sofa, one hand gripping the linen bandage on her forearm. She felt weak, drained, her head a boulder too heavy to lift. Earlier, the mederi had tied a length of cloth around Phoenix's forearm, making the blue veins swell up. Then the mederi had opened one of the veins with a lancet and let the blood trickle into a white bowl. Phoenix had been afraid that too much was spilling out, that she would bleed to death. The blood had smelled of iron. Now as Phoenix remembered, her stomach surged, and she feared she might be sick. The mederi had said it would take a few days for Phoenix to feel the benefits of the bloodletting.

Two long days passed, and on a rainy Songday, Mederi Gale came again.

"Do you feel any better?" she asked as she took off her wet cloak and hung it on the costume rack.

Phoenix shook her head.

"Hmm. I've thought of another treatment. Let's try shocking your system out of the Nethersea. We'll use two tubs of water—one hot, one cold. You'll plunge into one for five minutes, then into the other, hot to cold, then hot to cold again." She turned to Aunt Liona, who was staying home with Phoenix that day. "Do you have two tubs large enough for Phoenix to fit into?"

Aunt Liona nodded. "I'll start heating some water." As she did on bath nights, Aunt Liona placed pots of water on all four burners of the stove. Soon the windows steamed up. The mederi pumped bucket after bucket of cold water and poured them into one of the tin tubs until it was nearly full.

When both tubs were ready, Phoenix removed her clothes. She walked, her legs unsteady, to the tub of hot water, where steam curled up like misty white flames. As she bent down, tiny droplets clung to her face. She slid one toe in and wiggled it. The water felt hot but not scalding. She stepped into the round tub and sat down with her knees drawn up. Her back pressed against the tin on one side, her toes on the other side. The water covered her chest. As the heat enveloped her, she closed her eyes and yawned.

After five minutes the mederi said, "Now the cold water."

Phoenix stood up dripping, stepped out of the tub of hot water, and stepped into the tub of cold water. She forced herself to sit down. Daggers of cold seemed to slice into her body, and goose bumps rose on her skin.

"How long do I have to stay in here?" she asked, shivering, aching.

"Four more minutes," said the mederi. "I'm counting."

It seemed like forever, but when the time was up at last, Phoenix hurried to the tub of hot water. She submerged herself gratefully, reveling in the warmth.

But all too soon the mederi said, "Time for the cold again."

And so it went on for half an hour until the hot water had cooled.

"I think that's enough," the mederi said.

Aunt Liona handed Phoenix a big towel, and she dried off. Her fingertips had shriveled like prunes from being in the water so long.

"How do you feel, Phoenix?" the mederi asked.

"Cold," Phoenix said. "Awake. A little angry."

"Good!" Mederi Gale exclaimed. "Then you are not feeling so sluggish, or so full of despair. I think the treatment helped. Now we'll have to see if it holds. I'll be back tomorrow. But before I go, may I have pen and ink, please?" After she scribbled something down in a book covered with burgundy leather, the mederi left.

For an hour Phoenix lay on the sofa hoping to feel better, hoping and hoping. More than anything else in the world she wanted to feel better. She wanted to get back to the shop to make the shoes for the princesses. She forced her face into a smile, pretending happiness. But, as she traced her curving lips with one fingertip, she could feel the hope sliding downward, shooting down a dark shaft, down and down until it fell into the black mire inside her. The shadows of the Kingdom of Darkness still wrapped her in their shroud. She would be trapped with the gibbering skull in the curio cabinet forever. She slammed one hand against her pillow.

"What good did it do!" she shouted. "What good! All that blood and cold and for what?"

Aunt Liona came and hugged her. "There now, there."

"It will never go away, never! It's crushing me, Aunt, it's crushing me! Why? Why?" Phoenix turned over, crouched on her hands and knees over her pillow, and began to rock back and forth. "The mederi can't help me," she whispered. "No one can help me."

"I've left this as a last resort," Mederi Gale said the next day. "It's a new herb called laven's wort, which is very rare. It has recently been discovered high on a mountain on a remote island in the Southern Reach. I haven't used it yet, but scattered reports have come from the mederi working in the reach. Those reports make me suspect that the herb might lift people out of the Kingdom of Darkness." She held up the small bag of herbs. "There is some risk, but it may help you. Are you willing to try?"

"Anything," Phoenix said, blinking back tears.

"Laven's wort is a stimulant, and there's a chance it may send you straight into the Kingdom of Brilliance. But I'm hoping if I give you a small enough dose, that won't happen."

Phoenix nodded.

"Let me show you how to brew the herbs into a potion," the mederi said to Aunt Twisle. They went into the kitchen. Ten minutes later, Phoenix began to smell something nasty. Of course, she thought, of course the potion would smell nasty, and probably taste worse.

When Mederi Gale handed her the cup, Phoenix stared down at the dark green liquid inside.

"It looks foul," she said.

"It is foul," said the mederi, "but I think it will help."

Phoenix took a deep breath and drank the potion; it tasted of mustard greens, bark, boiled leather, and raw onion.

"You must take it every night," the mederi said. "We'll see what happens."

That night Phoenix turned one way on the sofa and then another, but sleep eluded her. The next morning she rose before her aunts were up. She went to the kitchen, lit the fire lying ready in the stove, then pulled out bowls, spoons, measuring cups, canisters of sugar and flour, tins of salt and baking soda, eggs, frying pans, and cookie sheets from the cupboards. She threw butter into a bowl and mixed it with sugar, beginning the dough for sugar cookies. When it was half finished, she grabbed another bowl and mixed flour, salt, and milk and began to make pancakes and waffles. She left the lids off the canisters and tins. She left the measuring spoons sprawled on the counters beside little spills of sugar and flour.

Aunt Twisle came into the kitchen. "Why, Phoenix, you're up, how wonderful!" Then she saw the mess. "What are you doing?"

"I'm making cookies, pancakes, and waffles," Phoenix said. "And I'm about to start sausages. I'm making a glorious breakfast for my darling aunts."

"Phoenix!" Aunt Twisle exclaimed. "We need this food to last the entire week."

"I know! We ought to invite the whole building. I'm feeling good. I'm feeling fine. The potion worked. Isn't it wonderful? I'm cured! May I go back to work today? I have to get started on the shoes for the princesses. I feel as though I could make all twelve pairs in one day. Quick as lightning. Oh, the pan is hot! Here go the pancakes. Sizzle, sizzle, sizzle. I hope you're hungry."

After she dropped the batter into the pan, she whirled around and cracked eggs into the waffle batter. She threw the shells over her shoulder. One hit Aunt Mulgaussy, who had come to stand beside Aunt Twisle in the doorway.

"Maybe I'll go out in a rowboat today," Phoenix said. "I'd love to row on and on. I wonder if I could row all the way around Faranor. Maybe catch a fish, ten fish. Wouldn't you like fish for dinner, darling Aunt Mulgaussy? We'll fry them in butter, with salt and pepper, oh, they'll be delicious with some new potatoes in parsley and—"

"She's in one of her flighty moods," said Aunt Mulgaussy, scraping off the eggshell.

"It's that medicine, that laven's wort." Aunt Twisle sighed. "I'll get dressed and go down and send a messenger to get Mederi Gale."

"No, no," cried Phoenix. "I'm fine! I'm cured. I'm not in the Nethersea anymore! The bees are buzzing inside me. This is lovely, lovely. Can I go to Harbor Road? Can I go to work? Oh, the pancakes need to be flipped!" She shook the pan and tried to flip the pancakes. They spun high into the air and landed on the floor.

"Whoops!" she cried. "Oh, well, there's lots more batter!"

By the time Mederi Gale arrived, Phoenix had baked three dozen sugar cookies, made a dozen pancakes, cleaned the front room, and through it all talked nonstop.

"I see that even a small dose of laven's wort was too much," the mederi said, watching Phoenix dust the curio cabinet with a duster in each hand. "I feared as much, but it was worth a try." She paused. "I wonder what would happen if I combined the laven's wort with some osalea—that's a calming herb. I've no idea how they will interact. Maybe the laven's wort would cut off her low moods, while the osalea would cut off the high moods. It's worth a try."

She wrote something down in her burgundy book. "I'll also decrease the laven's wort some. I'll go back to Healer's Hill and make up a new batch of the medicine. One of my apprentices will bring it down. Brew it the same way. Have her take it immediately, then once every night."

That night, full of the new potion, Phoenix slept well. In the morning she woke, yawned, and sat up. The bees that had been buzzing inside her yesterday were gone. Instead of being in the Kingdom of Brilliance, she had landed right back in the depths of her sadness.

"No," she whispered, "no." She would much rather be in the Kingdom of Brilliance than in the Nethersea. She loved the Kingdom of Brilliance, the early phase of it anyway, before she got wound up so tightly that she could not do anything.

Her stomach surged. She put one hand to her mouth, then leaped up and ran into the kitchen, where she threw up in the slop pail.

"Now I not only feel sad," she told Mederi Gale when she came that day, "I feel sick to my stomach as well."

"Oh, dear," the mederi said. "And no improvement at all?"

"Maybe a little."

"I have the formula for your potion written down here." Mederi Gale opened the burgundy book. "Let me see, I think I will try adding some dukesfoot to settle your stomach. And I'm going to increase the laven's wort now that the osalea seems to be keeping you out of the Kingdom of Brilliance. I'll send over a new batch of herbs. I'm sorry this is all trial and error, Phoenix. I'm working in the dark here."

For the next two days, taking the new potion, Phoenix

felt no better. Then, on the third day, she got up occasionally and wandered around the three rooms, her legs trembling from being in bed so long. The following day, she began to make sugar cookies again but left the dough half made because the wooden spoon felt as heavy as iron.

"But that's a good sign!" Mederi Gale exclaimed when she came on her daily visit. "You wanted to do something, even if you didn't finish it. And yet you're not in the Kingdom of Brilliance. I think we're making progress at last. This is exciting. If you continue to improve, I'm going to try this combination of herbs with my other patients."

Each night before she went to bed, Phoenix swallowed the potion her aunts brewed for her. As the days passed, first the fiery breath disappeared from the skull she saw sitting in the curio cabinet, then the skull itself disappeared and she saw only the empty shelf behind the curving glass doors.

12

Shoemaker to the Royal Household

ON THE SEVENTH DAY AFTER SHE had begun taking the new potion, Phoenix's aunts allowed her to go to work for a few hours in the afternoon. She had come a long way out of the Nethersea, and the crushing ache in her chest had lightened. She still felt nauseated from the potion, but only in the mornings.

Yet she hardly cared about all that she thought as she walked toward work, looking at everything: a dog chasing a blue ball; a man braiding his beard; the sun striking a tin can—it shone bright enough to be a princess's crown. What had the princesses been doing all this time?

When Phoenix reached the shop she found, to her surprise, that her shoe sketches were pinned all over the shop. All the journeymen and apprentices, even Alfred, came up to shake her hand and congratulate her on winning the contest.

"Did you see the window?" asked Whelk. Someone had repainted the fancy, scrolling lettering, only now it said:

Apprentice of Percy Snailkips,
Phoenix Dance,
Shoemaker to the Royal Household,
by Appointment to Her Majesty,
Queen Zandora
of the Royal House of Seaborne

Phoenix stared and stared, then reached out and touched the curving swoop on the *D* in *Dance*. She could just imagine what Rora would say when she saw the window. She had written another letter to Rora, who still had not answered the first one or acknowledged the blanket Phoenix had sent.

"Well, Phoenix," said Percy Snailkips. "I'm glad you're feeling better. Got your sole back on you, so to speak. Ha! You need to take it easy for a few days, your aunts say. But the princesses are clamoring for their shoes. I told them you were sick, and they'd have to wait. Which twelve shall we make first?" They walked along the wall, looking at the sketches, and chose twelve.

"I don't have the skill to make these, sir," Phoenix said. "And it would take me forever to make twelve pairs even if I did have the skill. I'm hoping, of course, that everyone in the shop will help?"

The shoemaker grinned. "Thought you'd never ask. And since you gave that old woman your shoes, here's a new pair for you." He handed her another pair of plain brown boots. "Now, I know you have a kind heart and all, but don't go giving these away, too. I can't afford to shoe every poor bare-foot soul in the city."

Essentially, the shop ran on as before, except instead of doing lowly tasks, Phoenix had real lessons in shoemaking, and she worked on bits and pieces of the shoes for the princesses. The shoemaker or the journeymen or Whelk taught her every step of the process of making shoes: cut-ting, stitching, lasting, and bottoming. Alfred had to wash the windows and do the errands again, protesting all the while.

Phoenix liked working with the rich silks, satins, and tap-estry fabrics better than working with the leather, which had to be soaked and coaxed into place; there was an entire room in the shop for cutting out hides. Over the next few days, Phoenix learned more than most apprentices did in two months. She was determined not to let her illness—or the nausea she felt from the potion—stop her from work-ing. Sometimes, however, she had to run out to the alley while her stomach heaved.

"A lesson on attaching heels today," said Whelk on Wa-terday morning after she came back from throwing up in the alley. "If you think you can stomach it." He grinned. Phoenix grinned back.

"Watch carefully," Whelk said, and began the lesson.

Phoenix liked the way his hands looked so strong and confident when he held the tools, liked the way his black hair slanted over his forehead, and liked the way he worked so hard to hide his limp. The feeling she was beginning to have for him seemed like a tender green shoot sprouting up through the earth. Phoenix was afraid to say anything about it or to show it, lest some heavy foot trample it down. She wondered if Whelk had a sweetheart. Sometimes she caught him looking at her, and her heart sang with the hope that he liked her as much as she liked him.

The next afternoon Phoenix was in the main room of the shop fashioning a purple velvet bow for one of the princesses' shoes when the door opened and two men swept in. Both wore long, flowing wizard's robes. One was of medium height and had a long white mustache that drooped down on either side of his mouth. The other, in a midnight blue robe, was tall and had a long black beard and one eyebrow that grew in a straight line above his hawklike nose. Phoenix recognized Fengal, Whelk's uncle.

"Welcome!" cried Percy Snailkips. "Welcome to my shop, gentlemen."

"Good day," said the man with the drooping white mustache.

"We heard that you make the finest shoes in the kingdom," said Fengal.

Whelk appeared in the doorway to the other room.

"Uncle Fengal?" he asked. "I thought I heard your voice."

"My nephew," Fengal said to the man with the mustache. "So this is where you spend your days. This is my colleague, the wizard Olstaff. Attend us, boy. We wish to order new boots."

"I can assist you," said Percy Snailkips.

"No," said Fengal, "let the boy wait upon us."

Phoenix saw Whelk bite his lip. She undid the velvet ribbon and started wrapping it again, so she would have an excuse to stay in the room and watch what was happening. The two wizards sat down. Whelk went down on his knees in front of them and removed their shoes. He drew patterns of their feet, took some measurements, and asked questions about what kinds of boots they wanted. Suddenly, in the middle of this, he looked up.

"Uncle," he said, "I'm asking you again. Won't you teach me to be a wizard?"

"What's that, boy?" Fengal said.

"Teach me to be a wizard. Like you. I've been studying on my own—in the Book Tower—but it's not the same as being taught by a real wizard. And if you taught me, I wouldn't have to go all the way to Honorath."

"Honorath!" Fengal laughed. "That's where I studied. What makes you think that exalted school would take a shoemaker's apprentice like you?"

"I have some ability, I think, Uncle. Some small talent. Please teach me. Please."

Phoenix cringed at the sight of Whelk begging on his knees before his uncle.

"I'm a busy man," Fengal said. "I have no time to waste teaching boys. I advise you to give up this nonsense. You have a perfectly good trade here as a shoemaker. Believe me, it's what you're fit for. I expect you to make our boots with your own hands."

Whelk's shoulders sagged.

"Now, if you're finished taking measurements," Fengal said, "help us on with our shoes and we'll be on our way."

After the two wizards left, Whelk continued to kneel on the floor, staring down at the papers with the outlines of the wizards' feet. Phoenix went up to him and put one hand on his shoulder.

"You don't need him, Whelk," she said. "You'll go to the school on Honorath. I know you will."

"It's just—" Whelk sighed. "It's just that I've wanted to be like him ever since I was little. He's one of the most powerful wizards in the kingdom. I've always looked up to him. Especially after my father turned out so . . ." He took a deep breath. "And yet he doesn't care a thing about me." Whelk seized the paper with Fengal's foot traced on it. "I wish I could tear this up," he said, waving it. "I wish . . . I wish . . ." He sighed again.

Phoenix squeezed his shoulder. "Let's get back to work," she said softly.

A week after Phoenix had returned to the shop, they finished the first batch of the princesses' shoes. On a bright

Landay afternoon, Percy Snailkips took Phoenix to the palace. Again, she wore Teeska's gold dress with the red undertunic.

"I want you to have the dress, Phoenix," the shoemaker said as they walked over a bridge in the Court of Canals. "It's the least I can do, seeing how you brought the royal appointment back to the shop."

Phoenix, pushing the handcart beside him, smiled and thanked him. It felt good to smile. It felt good to walk in the sunshine while the fan-tailed finches flew between the hickory trees with their new green leaves budding out. Most of the crushing weight of the Kingdom of Darkness had lifted from her, though she still tripped over some of its sad, lingering shadows. Since she had improved so much, Mederi Gale had stopped coming to see her every day. But Phoenix had an appointment to go up to see her at Healer's Hill on Moonday.

To Phoenix's surprise, the princesses remembered her.

"It's our own little shoemaker, Phoenix Dance," they said, gathering around her in their parlor. They looked thinner than before, and their eyes glittered.

"Remember how she laughed," said Princess Batissa, dressed in pale lemon-and-cream-striped silk.

Princess Coral tugged on her red hair, today worn long and loose. "We have been waiting forever for the shoes. It has been impossible, impossible! Being without them. Give them to us at once."

"We have had to wait because you were ill, Phoenix," said Princess Norris. "Is it true you have the Illness of the Two Kingdoms?"

"Yes," Phoenix said.

"Then you are mad," said Princess Batissa, stepping back. "Only crazy people have that illness."

Phoenix swallowed hard and rolled the handcart back and forth; the squeaky wheel creaked.

"Batissa!" Princess Osea exclaimed. "Your manners!"

"But it's true," said Princess Batissa. "One of our maids has it, and she tried to jump out an upstairs window. She thought she could fly. She broke her leg in three places. That is certainly mad. My premonition about Phoenix was true. There *is* something wrong with her!"

"A crazy girl should not be making our shoes," said Princess Tigrina.

"It does not matter whether she is crazy or not," said Princess Coral. "Just give us the shoes! We must have them."

Phoenix tensed her jaw, fighting to hold back the tears. Part of learning to live with her illness, it seemed, would be to endure jibes from others. She wanted to run from the room, but she could not leave without being dismissed.

"Why, I think she's going to cry," said Princess Myadora, who was gentle, silly, and slow.

"Maybe she's about to do something crazy," said Princess Coral.

"Do not torment her!" cried Princess Aurantica. "I forbid it. Think! Who are we to say what is mad?"

At that, all the princesses fell silent.

"I apologize for my sisters' rude behavior, Phoenix Dance," Princess Aurantica said. "Please forgive them."

Phoenix, her cheeks burning, bowed. She blinked hard.

"Come, Princesses!" the shoemaker said. "Won't you sit down? We'll unpack the shoes right away."

They all sat down. Their ladies-in-waiting removed the princesses' everyday shoes—white kid slippers full of holes. This time, instead of giving the princesses all their shoe boxes at once, the shoemaker doled them out one at a time.

"First, Your Highness Princess Aurantica," he said.

"No," Princess Aurantica said, "begin with Princess Batissa. I will go last."

"Very well." Percy Snailkips found the right box. "Phoenix, you will fit the shoes, please."

This time, as the princesses received their shoes, they did not dance but sat staring at their feet. Princess Coral stroked the lavender satin on the side of her shoe as though it were a cat. Princess Batissa cradled her shoes in her arms and rocked them back and forth, the ribbons streaming down the front of her dress. Princess Osea held her shoes against her cheeks.

When Phoenix had finished with all the other princesses, she knelt in front of Princess Aurantica. As the princess pulled up her skirt to expose her foot, her dark gray silk gown rustled, and shadows caught in the folds. Phoenix wondered why she always wore gray.

"I loved your sea slippers," the princess told Phoenix.

"When I put them on, I felt as if I could float away to a beautiful island. An island bathed in the rays of the sunrise—all pink and gold. I felt like the Sea Maid riding the waves in her scallop shell."

Phoenix smiled. "Then maybe you'll like these shoes, too." She held up the new shoes for the princess to see. Part of the Sea Maid's face was rendered in sequins on a dark blue velvet ground. Her red hair curled across the toes and around the heel. Phoenix had glued on the sequins one at a time; it had taken hours.

"How exquisite," the princess murmured, taking one shoe in her hands. As she looked at it, Phoenix looked at her. The princess seemed tired. Her skin was chalky, with lavender shadows smeared beneath her eyes. On the inside of her elbow the delicate skin looked blue and bruised. All of the princesses looked tired, and yet they were also glittery, brittle, and red-cheeked, as though they had a fever. Phoenix wondered if they were ill. But that would not explain why they were so obsessed with their shoes. Whelk had suspected there was magic involved with the princesses wearing out their shoes. Seeing them now, Phoenix thought he might be right.

"These shoes are too beautiful to wear," Princess Aurantica said.

"Will Phoenix be making your wedding shoes, Aurantica?" Princess Semele asked.

Princess Aurantica stiffened. "Yes, I suppose so." She gave Phoenix back the shoe, and Phoenix slipped it onto the princess's silk-stockinged foot. She had a high arch and long toes. Her feet smelled faintly of damp fur.

"Your Highness is betrothed?" Percy Snailkips asked. "What good tidings for Windward!"

Princess Aurantica did not speak. Phoenix, still kneeling on the floor, glanced up and saw the princess grip the arms of her chair and dig her fingernails into the gold velvet upholstery.

"We will all be bridesmaids at the wedding," said Princess Batissa, "all eleven of us. Phoenix, you will have to make special matching shoes for us all. Not yellow."

"Of course, of course!" the shoemaker cried. "When is the wedding?"

"In three months," Princess Norris said. "On the thirtieth day in the month of Long Days. When the roses are all in bloom."

"Only three months," Princess Aurantica said softly. Her head drooped forward.

Phoenix wanted to reach out and pat her cheek. Instead, she asked, "Will you walk in the shoes, Your Highness, to check their fit?"

Princess Aurantica walked across the room to the window, where she put one hand on the leopard's head and stood looking out. Her back was as stiff as the carved wooden figurehead on the ship *Aurantica*, now sailing somewhere far away on Windward's seas. As on the day Princess Aurantica had christened the ship, Phoenix felt the thread of sadness loop between them, but she did not feel it so powerfully as she had then. Instead of having her whole self share the well of Aurantica's sadness, Phoenix only dipped her hands into the water. This, she suspected, was thanks to the potion.

Everyone else in the room watched Princess Aurantica, too. The sun shining through the window made the sequin face on the side of her shoe sparkle, and for a moment it seemed as though the princess's face was on her feet.

"The shoes fit fine," Princess Aurantica said. "Everything is fit for a crown princess who must do her sworn duty, bitter as it may be."

13

Healer's Hill

ON THE TWENTY-SIXTH DAY OF THE blustery month of Blossom, the wind followed Phoenix as she hurried through the door of the long white building on top of Healer's Hill. She did not want to be late for her meeting with Mederi Gale. As she waited in line for directions at a long table, she looked at the paintings of flowers and seascapes hanging on the walls.

When at last Phoenix reached the front of the line, a boy in a blue robe gave her directions to the mederi's study. She walked down a quiet hallway with white walls and gleaming oak floors. Phoenix climbed up one flight of stairs, her fingertips gliding on the polished oak banister, then turned right and walked down another hall, where she passed several people dressed in white muslin robes like those Mederi Gale wore. People said the mederi practiced magic, but

Phoenix saw no evidence of that. She saw no one waving wands, heard no one chanting spells or muttering over crystals. Some people wore green robes. The younger people all seemed to be wearing blue.

When Phoenix came to a door with a placard that said *Mederi Cerinthe Gale*, she knocked twice.

"Come in," a cheerful voice called.

When Phoenix opened the door, she saw a burst of green. Plants filled the room, growing in pots on every surface—on the floor, along the mahogany desk, in between stacks of books on the bookshelf, and across the long narrow table against the far wall. Mederi Gale, dressed as always in a white muslin robe, stood pouring water from a blue watering can into a fern hanging in a pot suspended from the ceiling. Behind her, two windows stretching from the floor to the ceiling looked across a green lawn to the wind-bent fir trees on the bluff. On one corner of the desk stood a vase of daffodils with heavily ruffled double blooms. Above the narrow table hung a large painting of the Sea Maid riding her scallop shell, which six blue sea horses pulled across the waves.

"Welcome, Phoenix Dance," the mederi said. "Won't you sit down?" She nodded toward the two comfortable blue chairs sitting across from the desk.

Phoenix sat. "You must like plants."

"I do. These all have medicinal uses. We grow them in the herb garden and the big greenhouse in back, but I like having them nearby as well." She set the watering can on a stool and sat down behind her desk. "So, tell me. How are you feeling?"

"Better."

"The Sea Maid be praised. But?"

How had she known there was a but, Phoenix wondered. She looked at the vase of daffodils. Their ruffled faces were too heavy for their slender stems, and they bent over, drooping a little. That, Phoenix thought, was how she felt, a little droopy—not the terrible blackness of the Nethersea, not that anymore, thank the Goddess, but a little droopy.

"I'm out of the Kingdom of Darkness—mostly," Phoenix said. "But I'm still, I don't know . . ." She rubbed her neck, remembering how she had felt when she watched Princess Aurantica, as though both hands were submerged in a well of sadness. "I feel a little bleak," Phoenix added. "But it's nothing like before. I can get out of bed now, and I don't cry and hurt all the time. I don't want to . . . well, die either." Phoenix looked out the window, feeling her face grow hot with embarrassment. "I can't even remember why I wanted to. I've been working all day again, though I'm nauseated in the mornings."

Mederi Gale leaned back in her chair. "This is marvelous news, really. The medicine is working! We've stumbled onto something here. The persistent bleakness troubles me, though. Let's see what we can do about that and the nausea." She pulled out her burgundy book and flipped through the pages. "Yes, here you are. Let's see. Last time we added the dukesfoot for the nausea. Hmm." She reached for a large, thick book with gilt pages sitting on one corner of her desk and slid it toward her. Phoenix saw the word *Herbal* stamped on the cover in gold letters. Mederi Gale opened the book and turned the pages carefully. They were covered with illustrations of plants with text beneath them.

The mederi paused over a page. "Let's try teninger for the nausea instead of dukesfoot—it's stronger. As for the lingering sadness . . ." She turned more pages. "I might add a measure of surmoil. Sometimes that is used for those with melancholia. Or perhaps"—she flipped to the back of the book and ran her finger down a page—"perhaps woolswhip. Yes, I think that would be a better secondary herb to add to the laven's wort. Yes, let's try that." She closed the herbal and wrote in the burgundy-covered book. Then she leaned back in her chair. "In a little while we'll go down to the dispensary, and I'll make you up a fresh batch of herbs. But first, I'd like to talk about the warning signs of your illness."

"Warning signs?" Phoenix asked. "You mean like the pain in my chest or the bees buzzing inside me?"

"Yes. Things that you feel or do just before an episode of the Kingdom of Darkness or the Kingdom of Brilliance strikes. I want to see if there is a pattern of symptoms that could be clues that you're about to have an episode."

They talked about those for a while, the mederi scribbling down everything Phoenix said in the burgundy book.

"We must both learn to heed these warning signs," the mederi said. "The more we can observe about the illness, the more likely we are to find a way to treat it."

"How will learning to heed the warning signs help?" asked Phoenix.

Mederi Gale looked out the window at the wind-bent firs waving on the bluff. "I grew up on Normost, in the Northern Reach, where fierce storms batter the island. Imagine you are out in a boat and see a storm on the horizon. When will you decide to seek shelter and bring in your boat? Will you do it when you first see the storm clouds on the horizon? Or will you wait until you hear the thunder? Or wait until lightning bolts flash overhead?"

She looked back at Phoenix. "When do you realize an episode of the illness is coming on, and when do you decide to intervene? How many warning signs do you need? How intense must they be before you realize a relapse is happening? This is why you must heed the warning signs of your illness—watch for the storm clouds on the horizon. The earlier you can catch it, the better your chances of protecting yourself from the worst of the storm."

Phoenix frowned. "But why do I have to worry about all this if I'm taking the potion? Won't it keep me from having more episodes?"

"Taking the potion should help greatly, but I doubt it will be enough. You must also learn to watch your symptoms so you don't trigger an episode of the illness. Do you have any other questions?"

"I do," Phoenix said. "Why me? Why did I have to get this illness?"

"That is a question I can't answer."

"Did I catch it from someone?"

"No. The Illness of the Two Kingdoms is something you were born with, like your lovely red-brown hair."

"Why did the Goddess give it to me?" Phoenix asked.

"Again, I don't know."

"I don't want to be sick for the rest of my life. It isn't fair!"

"I know. But think of it this way. Nemaree the Great Mother also gave us the herbs in the medicine. And with the potion, if it continues to work, it's almost as though you're not sick. It's almost as though you're well."

"Can't you use your magic to make me well? Everyone says the mederi have magical healing powers."

Mederi Gale smiled. "I learned some magic during my travels in the Eastern Reach—bone weaving, blood stopping—but I'm afraid my powers are limited. I could use magic to make you calm when you are agitated—but the calm would last only as long as the spell—a few hours at best. I'm afraid there's no magic to cope with the Illness of the Two Kingdoms."

After they talked for a while longer, the mederi asked Phoenix to come with her to the dispensary, where she would make up the new batch of herbs for the potion. They walked down to the far end of the first floor.

"Are all the people in white muslin robes mederi?" Phoenix asked.

"Yes. The people in blue robes are apprentices. The ones

wearing green are healers—those with greater knowledge than apprentices but less than mederi."

A large room, the dispensary had rows and rows of shelves covered with blue and white jars. Each jar was neatly labeled with the name of the herb, root, bark, or mineral it contained. Waist-high counters held scales with suspended pans for measuring out the herbs. Also on the counters were beakers, tubes, and strange lanterns for heating liquids. One of the mederi's blue-clad apprentices fetched the jars she needed, but she measured out the ingredients herself, weighing them on the scales. She recorded everything she did in the burgundy book. When she finished, she gave the linen bag of herbs to Phoenix.

"Tell your aunts to brew this just as they did the last batch," the mederi said. "I'm very pleased with your progress. Keep asking difficult questions. Save them up for our next meeting in two weeks."

With the new potion wrapped in a bundle under her arm, Phoenix went straight from Healer's Hill to work at the shoemaker's shop. There, to her surprise, she found a letter waiting for her from Rora. At last. Phoenix broke the seal and read the letter, written in a tiny, slanting script.

Phoenix,
Here I am suffering for the noble Archipelagan cause in this dreadful prison, eating nothing but oatmeal, and I hear from my father that you have learned nothing from

my example. Nothing! Did you think I wouldn't find out that you are now Shoemaker to the Royal Household? You should have declined this honor *in my name, to PROTEST my imprisonment. I am DISAPPOINTED in you. I fear that the officials may read my mail or I would tell you why I am even more disappointed in you. I will only say that I* trusted *you, and YOU FAILED ME. I believe you may have done more than that. I believe you may have done something TERRIBLE. Sadly, all the evidence points to it. As I sit in here rotting, and you are outside, free, making frivolous shoes for frivolous people, I grow more FURIOUS every day. I guess since you have the misfortune to be descended from the nobility you will always be a ROYALIST at heart.*

Goodbye,
RORA

And that was all. No apology for the night at the Parliament Building. No regret for what she had done, or for the worry she had caused everyone through her recklessness, or for dragging Phoenix into danger. No mention of the blanket Phoenix had sent. Phoenix crushed the letter in her hand and dropped it into the rubbish can.

As she gathered rags and pumped a pail of water to wash the front window—poor Alfred needed some relief—she wondered what terrible thing Rora thought she had done. Was deciding not to commit a crime terrible? And what did Rora mean by writing "Goodbye," as though they would never see each other again? Rora would be out of prison soon. Well, they would make up then, Phoenix thought as she dunked a rag in the water. After all, they had been friends since they were little girls.

All in all, Phoenix decided as she scrubbed the window, her life was going well. She was feeling better; she was learning about her illness; she had helped make beautiful shoes for the princesses; and, best of all, she was Shoemaker to the Royal Household. How far she had come since the cold day she had stood outside this window looking at the sign *Apprentice wanted, inquire within.*

Phoenix had just finished washing around the beautiful scrolling lettering—puffing with pride as she wiped the rag carefully around her name—when she saw the royal messenger with a bag slung over his shoulder striding down the street. He opened the shop door. Phoenix stopped dead, clutching the rag, soapy water dripping all over her skirt.

"No," she whispered. Phoenix did not have to look inside the bag to know she had just lost the royal appointment.

14

Sirens and Proclamations

H AVE YOU HEARD THE NEWS?" cried Alfred, bursting in the front door of the shoemaker's shop three weeks later. He had been out running errands and had several bundles tucked under his arm. "Master Shoemaker Kilwarren's shoes came back this morning! The princesses wore them out, too."

Phoenix eased her foot off the leather stirrup that held the dancing slipper she was working on tight against her knee and ran up to Alfred. Everyone else in the shop gathered around him, too.

"That makes five shoemakers they've tried," Whelk said. "Master Snailkips, our own Phoenix, Mistress Smythe, Mistress Odark, and now Master Kilwarren."

"The queen can't say we're all making shoddy shoes," Percy Snailkips said. "The princesses are dancing their shoes to shreds every night, and that's the plain truth."

"But how are they doing it?" Phoenix asked. "The guards swear that they hear no sound, that the princesses are always in their beds, and—"

"I've said it before and I'll say it again," Whelk interrupted. "There's magic afoot."

Everyone except the shoemaker laughed at his pun.

"It's no laughing matter," the shoemaker said. "Something's wrong with our princesses. The palace servants say they sit around pale and sad all day long. Princess Aurantica takes no interest in the plans for her own wedding. It's unnatural, I say."

Phoenix wondered if the princesses had slipped into the Nethersea. She had come completely out of it, thanks to the latest batch of the potion, and she had managed to stay out of both the Kingdom of Brilliance and the Kingdom of Darkness. Although she had been sad and angry for a while after she had lost the royal appointment, she had not been thrown into deep grief. She worked every day, slept eight or nine hours every night, and her life felt as flat as her workbench. Phoenix knew the medicine was cutting off her high and low moods, but she felt squashed, repressed, as though she had no emotions at all. She did not like how she felt; she did not like it at all.

"I'd bet a gold piece that the princesses are enchanted," Whelk said. "Somebody's cast a spell over them. And I bet it's a wizard from the Order of the Black Dragon."

"The queen thinks so, too," Alfred said. "There was this

fine lady at the candlemaker's gossiping with the shop-keeper, see. Made me stand and wait they did. And this lady, she says the queen got a wizard who went to the school on Honorath to try to break the spell."

"Honorath?" Phoenix asked. She suddenly thought of the magic cloak the old woman had given her, which she had never taken out of her trunk because it could not help her make the most beautiful shoes in the kingdom, or win back the royal appointment, or get Trebonness back for her aunts; nor could it cure her illness or help her to live with it. Rora would be out of prison in two weeks, so there was no point in trying to use the cloak to free her. The Archipelago Party was planning a celebration on the day the prison officials released her.

"You'll never guess who the wizard is," added Alfred.

"My uncle Fengal?" asked Whelk.

"That was it," said Alfred, disappointed.

"I bet my uncle can break the spell," Whelk said, "if any-one can."

"Enough," the shoemaker said as a customer opened the door. "We have shoes to make, and they won't get made by gossiping or wizardry. Back to work, everyone."

Two hours later, when work was over for the day, Phoenix found herself leaving the shop at the same time as Whelk, which surprised her, because he lived there.

"Thought I'd take a walk," he said, falling into step be-side her, limping slightly. She slowed a little, smiled at him, then quickly looked away, pretending to be interested in some wild daisies growing beside the road.

"Going home?" he asked.

"First to Sea Dragon Courtyard," she said. "My aunts are usually dancing there this time of day. They catch the workers who want a little entertainment on their way home."

"Why don't I go with you and watch? I could use a little entertainment."

"Sure. If you want." Her heart was beating fast. "They're very good." From the corner of her eye, Phoenix saw Whelk looking at her, and she tried to suck in her stomach. Since she had started the potion, Phoenix had gained a lot of weight. She who had always been thin now looked merely plump, but if things went on this way, she would soon be fat. Also, pimples blistered her once-smooth forehead, chin, and cheeks—another unwanted effect of the potion. Mederi Gale had been surprised by both the weight gain and the pimples. She had guessed that they came from the laven's wort, since none of the other herbs had such effects. Phoenix felt so ugly she could not bear to look at herself in the mirror when she combed her hair in the morning. Whelk would never want her for his sweetheart now. Phoenix could not imagine why he was walking with her.

When Phoenix and Whelk reached Sea Dragon Courtyard, the Seven Sea Stars were just about to begin a dance. The jets of water bubbled and murmured around the bronze sea dragon, as though the creature were gurgling deep in its throat.

A tall, red-haired woman in a royal blue cloak walked across the cobblestones and spoke to Aunt Liona, who led the troupe.

"See that crest on the woman's cloak?" Phoenix asked Whelk. "She's a dancer with the Royal Company. I wonder what she wants."

Aunt Liona stood shaking her head at the woman. Then the woman held out a coin, and Phoenix thought she saw the flash of gold. Aunt Liona hesitated. She walked over and spoke to Aunt Mulgaussy, who nodded and started untying the ribbons on her dancing slippers—decorated with rosettes of silver ribbon that Phoenix had made. Aunt Liona went back to the red-haired woman and took the coin. The woman threw off her cloak. Beneath it, she wore black tights under a red dancing tunic that fell in a graceful skirt to her knees. She removed her shoes, pulled a pair of dancing slippers out of her pocket, and put them on.

"I don't believe it!" Phoenix cried, watching the woman tie the pink ribbons on her shoes. "They're going to let her dance with them! There's a huge rivalry between the street dancers and the Royal Dancers. That woman must have offered Aunt Liona a lot of money. But why? Come on, Whelk, let's get closer to the front."

The woman, who was neither old nor young, pulled a comb out of her hair; the locks tumbled down in long red waves to her waist. Her skin was as white as an eggshell. She looked like the painting of the Sea Maid in Mederi Gale's study.

The dancers began a ballet called *The Siren on the Rock*, which Phoenix had watched many times before. It was the story of a siren, an immortal creature half woman, half bird, whose beautiful song lured sailors to dash their ships upon the Siren Rock, a great black rock in the sea. Standing to the left of the dancers, a black woman sang the siren song in a low throaty voice that was dark and bright at the same time. Phoenix had always loved this story. She was enchanted by the idea of something being so beautiful and powerful that someone would risk destruction to experience it.

Usually Aunt Mulgaussy danced the siren because she was the best dancer in the troupe. This time, however, she sat out and watched the red-haired woman dance the part. And dance it she did. Phoenix had never seen extensions so high, balance so perfect, line so exquisite. The red-haired woman jumped as high as a man. Her pirouettes spun tight and fast, dazzling the eye. From the tilt of her head to the tips of her fingers, every movement was precise but flowed into the next.

Behind the dancers, the sea dragon in the fountain seemed to rear up, rising from the pool of water with its bronze wings outspread. It, too, seemed to lure the ship—played by Aunt Twisle in a billowy white dress—to its destruction. Aunt Liona and three others danced the undulating waves. The only man in the troupe, Thomask, played the captain who in his mad desire to hear the song sailed his ship closer and closer to the perilous Siren Rock.

"If I were the captain," Whelk whispered, "I'd order all my crew to plug their ears with cotton. I'd have them lash me to the mast of the ship, so I could do no harm, and then I'd unplug my ears and hear the song."

"It would drive you mad," Phoenix said with absolute certainty.

"No. I would be strong enough to resist it."

Phoenix found that hard to believe.

As the dance reached its climax, the red-haired woman's dancing grew to a frenzy. She twirled and leaped faster and faster, her red tunic streaming out behind her. The sun, reflecting off the water in the fountain, dappled the wings and body of the sea dragon with moving spots of light, which made it seem to quiver with life. When the woman leaped onto the rim of the fountain and did tour jetés along the curving edge, the dappled light played over her, too. For a moment, in her red tunic with her red hair whipping out, she seemed to be part of the sea dragon—its fiery breath come alive.

"Beautiful!" Phoenix whispered. She felt a touch of the excitement of the Kingdom of Brilliance, and she let it surge through her—out from her heart through her arms and her legs—grateful to have a few moments when she did not feel squashed and flattened.

Whenever the woman's red hair and tunic crossed Aunt

Twisle's billowing white dress, it seemed as though Aunt Twisle were on fire, as though the sails of the ship were in flames. Finally, with a wild leap, Aunt Twisle struck the Siren Rock. She spun, sinking slowly, until at last she and Thomask fell down dead as the waves danced over them. The siren—the red-haired woman—danced on, triumphant, leaping over their bodies. Then, with a wild high cry, the singing and the dance ended.

Applause rang through the courtyard.

"That was wonderful!" Whelk exclaimed, clapping hard.

After bowing with the other dancers, the red-haired woman put on her street shoes and cloak. Thomask, smiling his most charming smile, began to pass the black velvet top hat. Coins jingled into it faster than ever before. The Seven Sea Stars surrounded the red-haired woman, shaking her hand.

"Come dance with us anytime," Aunt Twisle said. "You don't need to pay."

"What's your name?" Aunt Liona asked.

"I am Elliana Nautilus of Faranor," the woman said.

"*The* Nautilus?" Phoenix whispered.

The Seven Sea Stars all bowed to the woman.

"The Nautilus is the greatest dancer in Windward," Phoenix whispered to Whelk. "Maybe the greatest dancer of all time."

"When I was a girl," the Nautilus said, "I often danced with the street dancers. Thank you for letting me do so again."

"It was an honor," Aunt Liona said.

"The honor was mine," the Nautilus said, and she walked away. Phoenix stared after her. She could not get the image of the ship with the fiery sails out of her mind.

"Who is your friend, Phoenix?" Aunt Twisle asked, smiling at Whelk. Phoenix introduced them. Whelk bowed politely.

"What a charming young man," Aunt Mulgaussy said. "Why don't you come home and have dinner with us?"

"Oh." Whelk hesitated. "Thank you. I'd like to."

Phoenix cringed inside. She did not want Whelk to see their shabby rooms. But then, she knew her aunts' conversation would be so lively, they would make him forget his surroundings. And probably his wits, too.

They all left Sea Dragon Courtyard. In the middle of the next block they approached the pillared sandstone building that housed the offices of the Lord Mayor. A broad flight of steps led up to it, and on the steps stood a royal messenger and a trumpeter.

"Let's go hear the news," cried Aunt Liona. And they pushed their way through the crowd that was gathering.

The trumpeter raised the trumpet to his lips and gave three short blasts. Then the messenger unrolled a scroll; golden tassels swung from the ends. He began to read:

"Hear ye, hear ye. Good citizens of Windward, hear this proclamation from Her Royal Majesty, Queen Zandora of the Royal House of Seaborne, Queen of all Windward.

Greetings to our good subjects. We ask for your help in a most grave matter. Whosoever may discover how the royal princesses are destroying their shoes and their health each night will receive the hand of the youngest princess in marriage—marriages for the older princesses have already been arranged. Furthermore, he will also receive the Duchy of the Islands of Trebonness in the Western Reach—"

"Trebonness!" Aunt Mulgaussy exclaimed. Several people shushed her as the messenger stopped and looked up, glancing around severely. Then he cleared his throat, jiggled the pom-poms on his sleeve, and went on.

"All contestants must be approved by Us. Hear ye, hear ye, these are the words of the queen."

After the trumpeter gave another blast, the royal messenger rolled up the scroll. Then they both walked down the steps and made their way through the excited crowd.

"Percy Snailkips will be happy," Whelk said. "This means his shoes weren't at fault."

"Mine either," Phoenix said. "I want that royal appointment back!"

"What does the queen mean, all contestants must be approved by her? Can anyone enter?"

"Are you going to try, Duke Whelk?" Phoenix asked.

He grinned. "I wouldn't mind. Not if the princesses are

as beautiful as they say. Are they? You've seen them. Imagine me, married to a princess!"

Phoenix nodded and turned her head away. She remembered how Aunt Twisle and Thomask had fallen down dead in the dance, destroyed by perilous desire. No one would ever risk destruction for her. It was princesses Whelk wanted, not her, with her pimply face, her thick waist, and her flat, boring self. Phoenix was beginning to hate the potion.

15

Rora's Accusation

THAT NIGHT PHOENIX DREAMED OF A ship plowing across a dark sea amid bones bobbing on the surface of the water. Painted on the side of the ship in glowing red letters was a name—*Phoenix Dance*. She was dancing on the prow to the music of the sirens' song as the sails burned red against the black sky. Flames crackled and hissed, running up the rigging. The Siren Rock loomed, but just as the ship was about to crash upon it, she woke.

Phoenix had the same dream almost every night for the next seven days. Then at last came the day she had been waiting for, the day that the doors of Five Towers Prison opened and Rora was set free. That night the Archipelago Party held a meeting in the Onxy Community Hall which was partly a celebration of Rora's release.

By the time Phoenix, Aunt Liona, and Aunt Twisle arrived at the hall, the meeting had already begun. They were late because they had tried to persuade Aunt Mulgaussy to come to see Rora. However, no matter how fond Aunt Mulgaussy was of Rora, she refused to participate in an Archipelago Party meeting. "Just give Rora my love," she had said, clicking her knitting needles as she worked on her Horace row. "And tell her I'll see her soon." Phoenix, who wanted everything to be perfect for Rora's homecoming, was disappointed.

Now, as they searched for a place to sit, Phoenix clutched a handful of wild bluebells that she had found in the alley and picked to give Rora. Phoenix craned her neck, looking all around; she could not wait to talk to her friend. Phoenix wanted to discuss how she felt about Whelk, how much she hated being fat and pimply from the potion, and how she felt so flat all the time. She wanted to talk about the princesses, the mystery of the worn-out shoes, and why the ship with the burning sails haunted her dreams. Oh, she wanted to talk about everything! Rora would understand Phoenix's feelings in a way that her aunts and Mederi Gale could not.

Phoenix and her aunts finally found seats on a bench in the back of the hall. Up on the stage, Fengal was interviewing a stately woman whose brown hair was braided in a coil so high it seemed as though she were wearing an overturned basket on her head. They sat in chairs before a blue curtain that hung like a piece of sky behind them.

"Elior Dawn," Fengal said, "do you find these principles

of peaceful resistance you have just described to us to be effective?"

"Extremely so," she said. "Let me give you an example. On the island of Ygall in the Southern Reach, the Lady Regor is a tyrant. She seized a piece of land, a common grazing land that had belonged to the Ygallans for hundreds of years. She wanted it to build a summer home. We called all the citizens to come unarmed and sit down on the land. Hundreds came. Old men and women. Children. Mothers holding babies. We sang songs, told stories. Lady Regor called out her soldiers, but they refused to shoot at innocent, unarmed people or even to forcibly move us."

"What happened?" Fengal asked, stroking his beard.

"We did this day after day until Lady Regor gave in and allowed the people to keep the land for grazing their sheep and cattle. This is the idea of peaceful resistance. Instead of using power for destruction, you use your power peacefully to bring about change."

"Let's turn the discussion slightly," Fengal said, "and consider how the Archipelago Party might use these principles in our struggle to gain a second House of Parliament."

As the discussion continued, Phoenix looked for Rora, but did not find her in the sea of hats and scarves. There must have been two hundred people gathered in the hall, and many had dark brown hair.

"Phoenix," Aunt Twisle whispered, "stop squirming. You'll see Rora soon enough." Reluctantly, Phoenix sat back in her chair and listened. After a few minutes, she became interested in spite of herself, liking what she heard. She did not think Elior Dawn would destroy statues. As Elior talked, Fengal shifted his feet beneath his dark blue robe. The toes of his boots showed, the boots Whelk had made for him, humiliated, hating each stitch.

When the meeting ended, everyone stood up and moved toward the tables in the back of the hall for cookies and tepid tea. Phoenix wandered through the crowd, her bouquet a bit limp, looking for Rora.

"If only one of us could discover how the princesses are destroying their health," a woman in a blue hat was saying, "then we would have an Archipelago Party member as a duke. Whoever holds the Duchy of Trebonness automatically becomes a Member of Parliament in the House of Islands. That would be another vote for our ideas."

"And how do you suggest we discover the secret?" asked a man. "Two princes and two knights have failed so far."

"I say the princesses should be stripped of their royal privileges," said a man with a pointed beard. "They aren't even doing their so-called charitable work anymore. They're not dedicating schools and buildings, or attending ceremonies honoring bright students or helping to raise money for worthy charities. No, they're too busy wearing out their shoes!"

The woman in the blue hat nodded. "And our taxes buy all those fancy shoes."

Phoenix, listening, felt anger ripple through her.

"Why aren't you worried about the princesses?" she asked

them. "Worried about their health and their state of mind? Something is terribly wrong with them. They're sick or under some kind of enchantment by the Order of the Black Dragon. You ought to be worried!" Without waiting for an answer, she moved on through the crowd.

"Well!" she heard the woman in the blue hat exclaim. But Phoenix had at last spotted Rora talking to Elior Dawn and three other people. Phoenix rushed up and threw her arms around her friend.

"Rora!" she cried. "I'm so glad you're back." However, Rora stiffened, and her arms stayed at her sides. Phoenix stepped back and held out the bouquet. "I brought you some flowers. Bluebells. Your favorite."

Rora neither took the flowers nor smiled. Her green dress hung on her; she had lost weight. Her golden brown skin did not have its old vibrant glow. As she looked Phoenix up and down, she slid her front teeth over the protruding mole beneath her lower lip.

"You've changed, Phoenix," she said at last. "Why, you're getting fat. And what in Nemaree's name has happened to your face? Have you quit washing it? I've never seen so many pimples."

Phoenix, still holding out the flowers, felt herself turning red as everyone looked at her. Slowly, she lowered her arms, speechless.

Rora turned to Elior Dawn. "This is Phoenix Dance. She's the girl I told you about. The one who has the Illness of the Two Kingdoms. The one who ran away before the

guards caught me that night at the Parliament Building."
Rora looked straight at Phoenix. "She ran away, and then
the guards came from the same direction she ran. You see
the connection?"

"Rora?" Phoenix clenched the bouquet; her fingernails
dug into the stems. "You don't think that . . . that I . . . ?"

Rora just stood with her eyebrows raised.

"I didn't call the guards," Phoenix said. "I would never—"

"Did you call them because you were sick in the head?"
Rora asked in a loud voice. "Were you crazy that night? My
father says your illness makes you crazy. If you admit you
were crazy that night, maybe I could forgive you."

"I wasn't crazy!" Phoenix exclaimed. "I'm not crazy."

"Then there's no excuse for what you did," Rora said. "I
trusted you. I won't make that mistake again. Go home,
Miss Shoemaker to the Royal Household. Make frivolous
shoes for your precious princesses while beggar children
roam barefoot in the streets."

"But, Rora, please—"

"Go home, I say. You don't belong here. You're a traitor."

Phoenix threw the bluebells on the floor. "I'm a traitor?
What about you? I trusted you. You never told me you were
planning to commit a crime that night. And you shouldn't
have done it either. What good did it do? It only got you
locked up in prison and made us all worry about you."

"It brought attention to our cause."

"It didn't help your precious cause one bit. It made people think of the Archipelagans as a bunch of hooligans."

Rora scowled. "You shut up. I spent extra time in prison because I wouldn't tell who was with me that night. I didn't betray you, and I could have."

"So you think you're some kind of hero? You're not. You hate the princesses, and you don't even know them. You could learn from Elior Dawn and do something besides smash statues!"

"Get out!" Rora shouted. "I don't want you here. This is my party. Now get out!"

16

Becalmed

THE NEXT DAY, THE TWENTY-FIFTH DAY of the month of Greening, Phoenix climbed the steep stairway up the side of Healer's Hill for another meeting with Mederi Gale. A quarter of the way up the hill, beneath a series of old oaks that arched over the path, Phoenix's legs began to ache. She could have taken a wagon up the road that wound up the hill, but she wanted to save the two shellnars it would have cost. It was late in the morning, summer at last, and not a touch of wind stirred the leaves on the oak trees. When she was halfway up the hill, Phoenix paused to wipe the sweat off her face and to look out at the spectacular view of Faranor.

Boats of every kind—coracles and pinnaces, schooners and frigates and sloops—sat becalmed on Majesty Bay, which lay as flat and smooth as a silver platter. There was not a sail in sight, only oars dipping and swooping like languid gulls flying low over the water. That, Phoenix thought, looking at the ships, was exactly how she felt—becalmed.

Inland, towers and domes reared up one behind the other: blue and peach; lavender and white; turquoise, green, and shimmering gold. To the north, Phoenix could see the palace, its four corner towers rising above all the others. She wondered if the princesses were wandering listlessly about their parlor, not eating, not playing their instruments, not plying their needles. Or perhaps they lay on their velvet sofas staring up at the ceiling with its painting of mermaids, sea monsters, and treasure chests floating in the swirling sea.

Farther to the north, the gray towers of Five Towers Prison bunched together. Phoenix scowled. As she climbed on up the stairs, which wound now beneath the waxy green leaves of overhanging camellia bushes, she fumed inside. How could Rora possibly have believed Phoenix would have betrayed her to the guards? And how could Rora have been so cruel—taunting Phoenix about the Illness of the Two Kingdoms in front of all those people? Phoenix brushed her cheek, feeling the pimply bumps with her fingertips. With her friendship with Rora severed, Phoenix felt as though a piece of her own body had been cut off, an arm or a leg set adrift on the sea. Strangely, though, this did not hurt so much as she thought it should have. She blamed that on the potion, which made everything seem flat and stale.

At last, Phoenix reached the top of the hill. She looked across a green lawn and saw the white building of Healer's

Hill stretch out before her. A long building, three stories high, it had rows of tall windows all along the sides. Today, most of them were open.

The two tall windows in Mederi Gale's study were open, too, when a few minutes later, Phoenix, sitting in the blue chair, breathed in the pungent smell of all the plants flourishing in the room. Phoenix told the mederi about the Nautilus, who had danced with the Seven Sea Stars two more times in the past weeks. Phoenix had been lucky enough to see her both times.

"When I watch her dance," Phoenix explained, "I feel . . . alive again. I never thought I'd get to see the Nautilus dance!"

Mederi Gale leaned forward in her chair. "What did she perform?"

"*The Princess and the Dragon* once and *The Siren on the Rock* twice. Have you seen her dance?"

"Oh, yes," the mederi said softly. "Many times. But I wonder why she's gone back to dancing in the streets. She hasn't done that for years now. She's almost forty, past the height of her powers. I should think she would be ready to retire. Dancing on cobblestones—she's destroying her body."

"When I'm watching her," Phoenix said, "I finally feel something. I've been feeling squashed, oh, I don't know, as though I'm living in a flat land, with no mountains or valleys. Like I'm living on a great gray plain that goes on and on the same forever as far as I can see."

"It sounds as if you're learning what it's like to live a normal life." The mederi dipped her pen in the ink bottle and wrote in the burgundy book. "One without extreme mood swings. This means the potion is working."

"This is what life is like for most people? It's boring!"

The mederi smiled. "Once you're used to it, I'd guess it won't seem so flat to you. But you'll probably always miss the excitement of the early phase of the Kingdom of Brilliance."

Yes, Phoenix thought, *yes*. But she didn't say it. Instead she reached out and touched a leaf on what looked like a lavender plant. "But I feel so much better. Are you sure I have to keep taking the potion?"

"I'm afraid if you stop, you'll slip back into the illness. Your illness is like your namesake, the phoenix. You cycle from ashes to flame, from darkness to brilliance, over and over again. The only thing I've found so far that can break that cycle is the medicine."

"Why can't I just take it when I'm sick?"

"Because I think the potion may prevent you from having more episodes. You see, the more episodes you have, the worse they'll get. So you have to take it all the time to prevent them from happening."

"But when I take the potion every night," Phoenix said, "it reminds me that I'm different from other people. That I'm sick."

"Try to think of it another way. The medicine is what keeps you well."

Phoenix shook her head. What the mederi said felt wrong, completely wrong. Phoenix looked at the corner of the mederi's desk where three old pieces of pottery sat in a row on a black lacquered tray. They looked like ancient drinking vessels—though only one had a handle. The cup on the left was blue, tall, and slender. The cup in the middle was brown, streaked with an orange glaze. The cup on the right—the one with the handle—was green and squat, and it looked as if it would fit comfortably into the hand.

"But I don't feel like myself anymore," Phoenix said. "It's like the potion has turned me into someone else." *Someone without the fire. Someone who is not completely alive.*

"You've lived all your life overshadowed by this illness," the mederi said. "Now you're discovering who you are without it."

The mederi looked at the painting of the Sea Maid hanging on the wall. "Once, a long time ago, I was confused about who I was. I believe that inside each of us there is a voice that knows who we are and what we should do. The trick is to find that voice, to listen for it, to hear it in the babble of all the other voices that fill us. I'm certain your real voice is in there somewhere, waiting for you to be well long enough so it can come out." She looked back at Phoenix. "But to find it you must give up the Kingdom of Brilliance. Forever."

"But I don't want to!" Phoenix finally blurted out what she had been feeling. She crossed her feet, uncrossed them, and then crossed them again. "After I saw the Nautilus dance

The Siren on the Rock," she said slowly, "I started having dreams about it. I see a ship with its sails on fire. All red and flaming against the black night. A ship with my name on it. It's, well, it's beautiful. Alive. That's how I want to be."

"But what about the siren's song?" Mederi Gale asked. "In the ballet it lures the ship closer and closer to the black rock, and the fiery song consumes the ship. I'd say the Kingdom of Brilliance is like the siren's song for you—a song of fire. It's something you long for, something beautiful and perilous that calls you. But as it does, you grow more and more out of control until the fire turns into a conflagration that threatens to destroy you."

Phoenix bent her head and put one hand across her eyes. "What if I learn to control it?"

"Oh, Phoenix," the mederi said, "do you honestly think you can do that?"

"Perhaps."

There was a silence.

"Do not forget," the mederi said at last, "never forget, that the Kingdom of Darkness lurks in the shadows."

Phoenix remembered how her white skull in the curio cabinet had gibbered like some kind of demon; how her chest had been crushed by the weight of a hundred stones; how she had wrestled with some loathsome thing, dredged up from the depths of the sea, its teeth sinking into her until she bled.

"I have one more question to ask you," Mederi Gale said. "Then I think we'll have talked enough for now."

Phoenix, her hand still across her eyes, did not move.

"Phoenix," the mederi said, "what color are your sails?"

Phoenix looked up. "What do you mean?"

The mederi's chair creaked as she leaned forward. "If you swept away the fire, the smoke, and the darkness, and saw instead the ship of yourself sailing in the light of a clear dawn, what color would your sails be? Who are you, Phoenix, at the heart of yourself?"

Colors swam into Phoenix's mind, but it seemed as though she saw them through a mist—yellow bled into green, which smudged into blue, which blurred into red. Not one stood out. Not one was hers. She looked at the cups on the mederi's desk, then looked away.

"I know this is all hard and new," Mederi Gale said. "Over the next two weeks, I'd like you to watch your emotions. See if they really are as flat as you think. Don't you still laugh and smile? Don't things still upset you?"

Phoenix nodded, thinking of Rora.

"I believe you'll find you have more of an emotional life than you think," the mederi said.

"I've gained even more weight."

"Try to watch what you eat. I know the potion makes you hungry."

"What about the pimples? I feel so ugly."

"I can give you some salve for the pimples. Come, I'll make it for you in the dispensary." The mederi stood up.

"I wanted to ask you about the princesses," Phoenix said

as they walked down the hall. "From what the queen said, it sounds like they're in the Kingdom of Darkness."

"They are."

"Are they taking a potion, too?"

"No. I've examined the princesses thoroughly, and a potion won't work for them because they're under an enchantment." She sighed. "The spell must be broken. Whoever learns their secret must find a way to break the spell and bring them out of the Kingdom of Darkness. I hope it's soon. The princesses are not well, and they're getting worse every day." Mederi Gale paused, then added, "People can die in the Kingdom of Darkness."

17

Racing with Seagulls

VERY DAY THE FOLLOWING WEEK the rain poured down, and every day Phoenix stitched and cut and glued and hammered, and her life felt as flat as the pancakes that Aunt Mulgaussy made for breakfast. Phoenix hated the way she felt, so trudging, so stale, like week-old bread. She was tired of living on the great gray plain, tired of feeling flat and squashed, tired of pimples and fat. Phoenix wanted to feel alive, alert, creative, full of fire. She could not give up the Kingdom of Brilliance, no matter what the mederi said. Besides, she felt so well now. Surely she did not need the potion anymore. It had made her well; it had made her strong. Its work was done. So, instead of drinking the potion, one night when her aunts were not looking she threw it into the slop pail in the kitchen.

As Phoenix held the empty cup in her hand, she heard

the mederi's voice in her head saying *People can die in the Kingdom of Darkness*. But not her, not her. The princesses. Phoenix wished she knew how to help them, Aurantica, Batissa, Osea, and all the others. She hoped Fengal would break the spell soon.

After work on Moonday, when she was folding her leather apron, Whelk came up to her.

"Can I walk you home?" he asked.

"Oh," she said. "Sure."

"Lovebirds," said Lance, grinning from ear to ear. "Aren't you sweet."

Phoenix felt herself turning red. She and Whelk left the shop, talking about the day's work, and soon found themselves on Harbor Road. The rain had stopped, though clouds burgeoning overhead threatened to burst again at any moment. They walked slowly, looking at everything. Phoenix was entranced by a man who swallowed fire on a stick.

"How does he do that without burning himself?" she asked Whelk.

"There must be some trick to it," Whelk said, and they walked on.

Every day that week, Whelk walked her home after work. On Landay, they lingered in the market again, watching a puppet show in which a dragon fought with a wizard. The wizard won. Afterward, Whelk bought her a brickly-brick sweetie stick from a candy vendor. Its sweetness melted on her tongue. On Waterday, they walked down to the ship-yards and watched men building a schooner. The sounds of hammering rang through the air. They toured a warehouse where sailmakers were sewing sails—purple, red, white, yellow, blue—almost every color there was. Phoenix thought of what Mederi Gale had asked her about the color of her sails. As the sailmakers stitched, they talked about the Order of the Black Dragon, which, in spite of the efforts of the Royal Navy and the High Council of Wizards, had seized more ships in the Belica Straits.

On Songday, Phoenix and Whelk climbed to the gardens on the hill to the east of the city, and tried to see who could spot the ships farthest out. Whelk won. On Fireday, Whelk took her hand, and a little shiver of joy ran from Phoenix's feet to her head as she squeezed his hand back. She felt the gentle weight of the carving of Ethalass pressing against her breastbone and the slight pressure of the cord against the back of her neck. Phoenix wore the carving every day, not because she believed in its protective powers but because Whelk had given it to her.

On their walks, she learned a few things about him, too.

"Where is your mother?" she asked him.

"Dead. She died a few months after my father . . . after my father was hung. I had just been apprenticed to Percy Snailkips. Then after she died, because my uncle wouldn't take me in, I came to the shop to live."

"No other relatives?"

"Only Fengal. At least I can be proud of him. I know he'll break the spell the princesses are under. I just know it."

"Why do you want to be a wizard?" Phoenix asked.

Whelk did not speak for a minute. At last he pointed to a gull swooping across the sky.

"It's like that gull there," he said. "Imagine being able to call it to your hand. Or speak to it, or understand its thoughts. That's why I want to be a wizard. To know the secret heart of things."

At night Phoenix lay awake, partly because she had not taken her potion but also because she was thinking about Whelk. She thought about his hands, how capable they were, stitching a sole onto a shoe, fashioning a bow for a latchet. She thought about his black hair slanting over his eyes. She thought about the way his shoulders curved as he sat at his workbench. Then she hugged her pillow, imagining it was him, and hoped it would be a long time before he saved up enough money to go to the wizards' school on Honorath.

As the days passed, and Phoenix only pretended to drink her potion—pouring it into the slop pail, out the window, or into the plants—to her joy she felt herself filling with the fiery delight of the early phase of the Kingdom of Brilliance. The world seemed to come alive. The roses growing everywhere in the city dazzled her, their colors—red, pink, yellow, gold, and white—sang out to her as she passed them. The borders on the awnings hanging from the shops fluttered in the breeze, dancing. And the smells! Good and bad, smells filled her nose—the sharp vinegary smell of the sea that blew up through the city streets, the sweet smell of the strawberries in the fruit vendors' stalls, the yeasty smell of the beer flitting out from the alehouse doors, and the golden smell of bread rising from the bakers' shops. Even the sounds—the shouts and laughter of the people, the horses trotting by, the carriage wheels creaking, the shop doors opening and slamming—seemed like music to her. She loved it all.

At work she went up to Percy Snailkips.

"I have some ideas, sir, lots of ideas for shoes, that I've thought of in the past few days. Some of them I think are pretty fine. May I have some paper and use the colored chalks? I won't use too much paper this time. I'll work small, you'll see, sir. I've got an idea for snakeskin shoes with jet-black beads and—"

"Fine. Certainly," said Percy Snailkips. "You may have one sheet. A bit lit up again, aren't you? Have you been taking your potion?"

Phoenix hesitated, then lied, "I've been taking some."

"Hmm," he said. "Well, see that you start taking it all or you'll soon be fit for nothing."

Phoenix found the paper and colored chalks and took them to her workbench. Her hand trembled as she began to draw. She drew snakeskin shoes with jet-black beads. She drew silver shoes with lacework latchets. She drew shoes with jeweled heels; shoes with black velvet ribbons and diamond buckles; shoes with golden cords wrapped around the toes; shoes with embroidered tongues, their sides ivory satin; shoes of red and gold, black and white. As she drew, the fire burned inside her, and her hand moved faster and faster. She was elated, happy, flying on the threshold of the Kingdom of Brilliance.

When the paper was filled up, she flipped it over. Laughing, she turned the charcoal on its side and with her whole arm moving in circles drew a huge heel that looked like the body of a sea dragon. Next, she drew the rest of the shoe. Then she added wings sweeping up from each side. A mouth gaped through the open toe, and a great tongue stuck out. With swift black strokes rising from the throat of the shoe, she sketched the long neck and head of a sea dragon. The monstrous shoe took up the entire page—two feet by two feet.

Finally, she drew flames streaking from the sea dragon's mouth. Red fire poured out in every direction, dancing, snaking, reaching to the edges of the paper. Phoenix put one hand against her heart to contain the sudden pain in her chest and smeared red chalk all over the front of her apron.

"That is beautiful, Phoenix," Whelk said. "And terrifying. Like something from a dream or a nightmare."

Phoenix laughed. "I don't think the princesses would want to wear sea dragon shoes."

"How about if I walk you home?" It was Landay, when they were dismissed early.

They took off their aprons, Phoenix chattering away, and left the shop together.

"Stop talking so much, Phoenix," Whelk said after they had walked three blocks. "I can't get a word in edgewise. Are you sick again?"

"No, no! I'm feeling fine. Lovely. I love the way I feel. This is how I want to feel all the time. I feel as though I could do anything. Whelk, do you want to kiss me?"

"Do I—" He stopped and looked at her.

"Haven't you wanted to kiss me for a long time? Haven't you? Don't you?"

"I guess so."

Phoenix clasped her arms around his neck. Whelk looked a bit startled, but he put his arms around her and kissed her. His lips felt rough. Phoenix did not know what to do with her head, how far to tilt it, and her nose seemed to get in the way. But the fire inside her burned more brightly.

"Lovely! Lovely!" she cried. And she broke away from him and ran.

"Wait!" he called. "Stop! You know I can't run. Where are you going?"

"I have to run!" Phoenix called. "If I don't, I'll burst!"

"But—"

"Goodbye! I'll see you tomorrow. I must run! Run and run and run!" And she did, she ran to Harbor Road, darting through the market, stopping only, on impulse, to steal a brickly-brick sweetie stick from a vendor's stall. She had not stolen anything since she was six years old.

She passed a group of actors putting on a skit. A man with a black hat and a long drooping mustache swaggered around, making the audience laugh. Phoenix laughed, too, louder than anyone else, until people began looking at her. When the skit ended, Phoenix ran to the shop that sold silk from the Eastern Reach. There she lingered, entranced by the vibrant colors—turquoise, pink, purple, and scarlet. She imagined herself swathed in a dress of watermelon-colored silk, dancing wildly.

Next, Phoenix came to a corner where a troupe of jugglers threw hoops and balls high into the air. She stared at the orange balls so intently that she felt she became one of them. She imagined the air rushing by her face, felt the tension inside as she feared the jugglers might drop her to the ground, where she would surely shatter. She ran on, not knowing where she was going, not caring.

When Phoenix reached Parliament Square, she found it filled with row upon row of people—there must have been over a thousand—who were all sitting down on the cobblestones. Guards with sabers watched from the edges of the square. Standing on the front steps of the Parliament Building, facing the crowd, were Elior Dawn, Rora, and Fengal.

"My friends," Elior was saying, "we, the members of the Archipelago Party, have come together today in peace and unity to show the queen and the Members of Parliament our wish for a second House of Parliament to better represent the people of this great kingdom. No violence will be done here today. We wish the power we show by our numbers to lead to productive change. We advocate change through peaceful methods. Are you with me?"

Everyone cheered. Phoenix, standing at the back of the seated crowd, cheered with them, as loudly as she could, and jumped up and down, too. Again, people glanced at her. Rora saw her, and they stared at each other across the square. Then Phoenix looked at the statues of the faceless princesses; no one had yet repaired them, if, indeed, they could be repaired.

Rora stepped forward. "As head of the Dolphins, I urge all the younger members to follow Elior Dawn's principles of peaceful resistance as we seek a change in our government."

Phoenix blinked. She could not reconcile this image of Rora with the one from three months ago. Here was Rora standing in broad daylight in front of everyone with the sun shining down on her. Three months ago, she had been skulking around this square in the dark with a hammer, smashing statues. Was this the same person? What had changed her? How had she brought her power from the dark into the light? Phoenix thought she knew the answer to that: Elior Dawn. And perhaps prison.

Elior began talking again.

"Sit down and listen," someone whispered to Phoenix. Phoenix, however, was far too full of buzzing bees to sit and listen to anyone talk. She turned and ran through the streets again, longing for Rora. She wanted her best friend back.

On the beach at the southern end of the Market District, Phoenix raced below the seagulls as the sun set, delighting in their whiteness, in their gliding flight. All the sights, colors, and impressions of the last few hours, the last few days, gathered together inside her, rolled into a ball of excitement like a kaleidoscope, shifting, turning into ever more spectacular patterns. Phoenix wanted to dance, to fling out her arms and sing and shout. She felt alive again, reveling and burning in the Kingdom of Brilliance.

At home, her aunts took one look at her and brewed the mederi's potion.

"But I don't want it!" Phoenix cried. "I don't want to live on that gray plain again. I want the fire! I'm strong enough—I don't need the medicine."

"We insist that you drink this," said Aunt Twisle, holding out a steaming blue porcelain cup. "And tomorrow we must bring Mederi Gale here to see you. You're ill."

Surrounded by her aunts, Phoenix took the hated cup and drank the wretched potion all in one gulp. Then she threw the cup on the floor, where it shattered into pieces.

"It makes me dull!" she screamed. "It makes me fat and ugly! I hate it! I hate it!"

18

Losing Whelk

PHOENIX SPENT THE NEXT FEW DAYS resting on the sofa with no stimulation at all; one of her aunts stayed home with her each day to make sure she rested. Mederi Gale did come, but she only looked at Phoenix soberly and said she must keep taking the medicine if she wanted to be well. So Phoenix's aunts brewed the potion for her each night and, ignoring her cries and pleas, made certain she drank it. "The great-granddaughter of Seagraine Dance does not fuss over taking her medicine," said Aunt Mulgaussy. Phoenix passed the time thinking about Whelk, wishing he would come to visit.

Finally, on the eighth day, when Phoenix was feeling flat and dull again, her aunts allowed her to return to work. She sat at her workbench doggedly punching awl holes into the leather sole she was attaching to a sturdy working man's boot. Again, she felt as though she were trudging along on the great gray plain again, and she loathed it.

Phoenix was grateful to be working once more, however. Earlier, she had tried to sketch some shoe designs, but they lacked fire and beauty, and it had taken her hours to work out details that had taken only minutes a short while ago. The results seemed dull. How she missed the Kingdom of Brilliance! Phoenix sighed and punched another hole.

For the third time Whelk passed her workbench without saying a word. He had not spoken to her all morning.

"Whelk," she said.

He stopped, turned, and slowly came back to her.

"Hello," he mumbled. "Are you feeling better?"

"I was feeling better before!" she snapped. "But everyone insists that I take the wretched potion."

Then, remembering how she had thrown herself at him, urging him to kiss her, Phoenix felt her cheeks grow hot. How could she have acted so brazenly? No wonder he seemed cold.

"You've calmed down," he said. "That's good."

She did not say anything. The front door opened with a creak, and Teeska, Percy Snailkips's fifteen-year-old daughter, came into the shop. A slender girl, she wore her blond hair in two braids twisted up on either side of her head. Her eyes were as blue as the sea. Her smooth white skin had three tiny freckles to the left of her nose.

"I baked you some cookies, Whelk," she said, holding out a plate.

"Thanks," he said, taking the plate.

"They're gingersnaps."

"They smell good," Whelk said.

"Are we going to take a walk again when you get off work this evening?" Teeska asked.

Again? thought Phoenix.

"I thought we could go over to Harbor Road," Teeska added. "I'd like to see the puppets."

"That sounds fine," Whelk said.

"Well, I've got to get back. I'm helping Mummy with lunch. I have so many responsibilities." Teeska adjusted the lace-trimmed collar on her dress, then turned and walked out of the shop. Whelk stared after her.

"Isn't she pretty?" he said to no one in particular. Then he turned to Phoenix and held out the plate of cookies. "Have one?"

"No, thank you," Phoenix said. She punched another hole into the leather sole so hard she hurt her finger. "Blast!" She glared at Whelk, who was offering cookies to the others.

Phoenix wanted to seize the plate of cookies and hurl it across the room. Only a week ago, Whelk had kissed her. Now he was seeing Teeska, and Phoenix thought she knew why. Because the potion made her boring. Because she had thrown herself at him. Because of her fat stomach and her ugly face covered with pimples. She blinked back tears.

"Phoenix!" called Percy Snailkips. "Come measure this fine young lady's foot."

At lunchtime, miserable, Phoenix went out into the alley. She remembered the day she had stood searching for treasures in the trash. How simple her life had seemed then. How bright and bubbly she had been before she had started taking the potion. And Rora had still been her friend.

The back door creaked, and Whelk came out with a flour sack filled with trash.

"Phoenix," he said, startled. "What are you doing out here?"

"Getting some fresh air," she said.

"Here?"

She did not reply, and he put the trash in the rubbish can. The lid clattered. Then he stood beside her.

"What's the matter, Phoenix?"

"I thought you . . . I thought we . . . liked each other. But now you're walking out with Teeska."

"I did like you," Whelk said. "I liked you a lot. Until the other day."

"What did I do the other day? You mean, because I kissed you?"

"No, because you ran. Listen, you know I can't run, and you just ran off and left me standing there. How do you think that made me feel?"

She did not say anything.

"Well, I'll tell you. It made me feel like a cripple. When you're sick you don't think of anyone but yourself."

"I know why you don't like me anymore," Phoenix said.

"It's the potion, isn't it? The fat and the pimples. How dull I am."

"It's just that you're a handful, Phoenix. The potion, your moods, the Illness of the Two Kingdoms. Listen, I never know where you are from one day to the next. Some days you're fine, other days you're on fire and wound up and talk too much, other days you're in the Nethersea. With Teeska it's easier. She's usually happy, and she's easygoing. You're just too much for me."

"Please, give me another chance, Whelk, please."

"I don't think so. Teeska's fifteen, like I am. We have more in common. I'm sorry."

But I love you, Phoenix wanted to say. Instead she said, "Fine. That's just fine." And she marched back into the shop and slammed the door. Inside, she slipped the carving of Ethalass off over her head and threw it on the woodpile by the stove. Now she had lost Whelk because of her illness. How much more of her life would it ruin?

19

A Bold Idea

I CAN'T BELIEVE MY UNCLE FAILED!" Whelk exclaimed in the shop three days later. "I just don't believe it! Are you sure your aunts heard right, Phoenix?"

"I'm sure," Phoenix said as she stitched tiny white beads along the throat of a high-heeled shoe. "They heard it last night at the Archipelago Party meeting. Fengal spent weeks trying to figure out the princesses' secret. But he couldn't find it out or break the spell they're under." Phoenix felt a little gleeful telling Whelk this, out of spite for his abandoning her for Teeska. "The queen has replaced him with Olstaff, the other wizard you made the boots for."

"That makes five knights, two princes, and one wizard who couldn't learn the secret," Alfred said.

Lance, who was cutting shoelaces from a piece of leather, looked up. "I heard that Master Shoemaker Egret has orders to make plain white kid slippers for the princesses. They wear them out every night. Then he makes up a fresh batch every morning."

"Corns and bunions, what a disgrace!" said Percy Snailkips as he walked by carrying a rolled-up hide. "Plain and simple slippers for princesses. Not a speck of decoration. They might as well be worn by the kitchen maids! But I can see why the queen doesn't want to pay for better."

"Listen, I still don't believe it," Whelk said. "My uncle is one of the most powerful wizards in the kingdom. If he can't discover the secret and break the spell, no one can. It must be the Order of the Black Dragon that has cast the spell over the princesses. No one else could be powerful enough to thwart my uncle."

"Fengal hasn't given up," Phoenix said. "My aunts heard he's studying the old scrolls in the Book Tower searching for a clue to break the spell." She prayed to Nemaree that he or Olstaff would find the answer soon. Mederi Gale's warning that people sometimes died in the Kingdom of Darkness kept running through her head.

"I wonder who will try to discover the princesses' secret next," Lance said. "Maybe someone ordinary should try. Someone with common sense, instead of knights, princes, and wizards. A farmer or a fisherman, or heck, why not a shoemaker?"

Everyone laughed.

As Phoenix picked up another tiny white bead and slid

her needle through it, she thought of the magic cloak the old woman had given her, still lying in the bottom of her cedar chest. It would certainly help anyone trying to discover the princesses' secret. Perhaps she should give it to the wizard. Then Phoenix's hand stopped, holding the needle in midair. Why shouldn't she use the cloak to try to discover the princesses' secret herself? She could win Trebonness back for her aunts! And instead of asking for the hand of a princess in marriage, she would ask for the royal appointment back.

Phoenix sat up straighter. If she did discover the princesses' secret, and if she broke the spell that trapped them in the Kingdom of Darkness, wasn't it possible that she might use what she learned to manage her own illness better—without taking the awful potion? Whatever saved the princesses from the Kingdom of Darkness might save her from it, too. The needle trembled in her hand, and the beads blurred before her eyes. Phoenix had not felt so excited since before she had begun taking the potion again.

But would Queen Zandora allow a girl and a commoner—although a commoner descended from aristocracy—to try to discover the secret? There was only one way to find out.

When work was over for the day, Phoenix found some paper, trimmed a quill, and wrote a note to the queen asking for an interview regarding the princesses' secret. She wrote the note three times before she was satisfied with it.

She signed it "P. Dance." After the ink dried, she folded it, addressed it, sealed it, kissed the seal for luck, and then delivered it to the palace on her way home.

That night, for the first time in days, her aunts did not watch her like a hawk as she drank the potion. Phoenix decided to try drinking only a quarter of it. Maybe that way she could stay on the threshold of the Kingdom of Brilliance without being pulled into its mad heart. Deep down, Phoenix knew if she followed this plan, she risked sinking into the terrible Nethersea in the Kingdom of Darkness or the frenzied madness of the Kingdom of Brilliance. But if that happened, she reasoned, she would simply start taking all the potion again. Of course, Mederi Gale had warned that Phoenix could not take the medicine only when she was ill. If she did, each episode of the illness would grow worse, harder for the potion to counteract. But she would worry about that when it happened. So she drank a quarter of the potion and poured the rest into Aunt Mulgaussy's jade plant.

Six days later, at eleven o'clock on a sunny morning, Phoenix went around to the tradesfolk's entrance to the palace to present herself for her meeting with the queen. She wore the gold dress that Percy Snailkips had given her, though it was tight in the stomach and hips because of all the weight she had gained. While Phoenix waited in a parlor, running her fingers over her bumpy cheeks—the salve

Mederi Gale had given her had not helped much yet—she began to have second thoughts about her plan. After all, she did not know a speck of magic. What made her think she could break the spell or even discover the secret when so many others, including a wizard, had failed? True, she had the magic cloak, but the magic she was facing was probably stronger than the cloak's magic. What if it did not hide her well enough? Phoenix swallowed hard and kicked one foot against the rung of her chair. If only she could talk to Rora about all of this.

Last night, Rora had been leaving Sea Dragon Courtyard just as Phoenix had entered it—Rora had ignored her. Would Rora ever apologize for the awful things she had said during their terrible argument in the Onxy Community Hall? Would they ever be friends again? Phoenix kicked the chair once more.

"P. Dance?" a footman called. Phoenix took a deep breath, stood up, and tried to smooth her dress; in spite of her efforts, however, it rumpled over her stomach. Pursing his lips, the footman eyed her doubtfully and then ushered her through a door.

The footman led her not to the throne room that she had heard so much about and had hoped to see but to a drawing room with walls covered in blue moiré silk. The woodwork was painted white, as was the crown molding around the ceiling. Queen Zandora sat in a high-backed chair upholstered in midnight blue velvet; its arms and legs were gold.

To the queen's right, slightly behind her chair, stood a lady-in-waiting in a lavender dress with a white lace collar that bristled into two crisp points.

"Your Majesty," the footman said, "may I present P. Dance."

The queen's eyebrows rose above her silver-rimmed spectacles. As Phoenix curtsied, she saw her letter lying open on a round marble table beside the queen's chair. Next to the letter were a glass, a crystal pitcher, and a stack of immaculately starched and pressed lace-edged linen handkerchiefs six inches high.

"A child, a girl, and a commoner!" the queen exclaimed. "P. Dance indeed. What is your name, child, and no nonsense."

"Phoenix Dance of Trebonness, Your Majesty. And if men, aristocrats, and wizards can't discover the princesses' secret, perhaps a bold girl is just what you need."

The queen stared, then her face softened, and she laughed.

"I think you may be bold enough to find out anything," the queen said. Her fingers twisted an emerald pendant that hung upon her breast. She was dressed all in shades of green satin, like the sheen on the sea when the sun strikes it slantwise through the clouds. Her shoes were green satin, too, embroidered with leaves and flowers, and fastened with rhinestone-studded buckles. Phoenix wondered who had made them.

"But this is absurd, child," the queen said. "I obviously

cannot offer you the hand of my youngest daughter in marriage. So tell me, why do you wish to try to discover my daughters' secret?"

"For three reasons," Phoenix said. "First, because I want to help the princesses. Is it true they're sick?"

The queen nodded. "All day long they are sad and still. Before this trouble began, my daughters sang, they sewed, they played the harp and harpsichord. They made things. They painted pictures—Princess Aurantica was a rather remarkable landscape painter. Now they do nothing all day long. They refuse to fulfill their obligations and appear in public. Nothing interests them—except their shoes. And they do not eat enough to keep a bird alive. They are wasting away." She took one of the lace-edged handkerchiefs from the stack on the table and pressed it to her lips.

"I'm sorry," Phoenix said. "I know how painful the Nethersea can be. And I'd like to help them come out of it. Especially Princess Aurantica."

The queen dropped the handkerchief on the floor. The lady-in-waiting picked it up.

"Princess Aurantica should be learning to attend to affairs of state," the queen said, "and she refuses. How will she run the kingdom one day?" The queen sighed. "I rule an entire archipelago, with hundreds of wise men and women, learned scholars and wizards and mederi all at my command. Yet not one of them—not one!—can tell me what is wrong with my beautiful girls. An enchantment, they say.

A spell cast by the Order of the Black Dragon. But they cannot break the spell, and meanwhile each day I think my heart can break no more and yet each day it does." Queen Zandora plucked another handkerchief from the stack and dabbed at her eyes.

Phoenix did not know what to say but stood silently, her heart filled with sorrow for the queen. The lady-in-waiting poured a glass of water from the crystal pitcher and handed it to the queen, who dropped the handkerchief on the floor and then drank. The lady-in-waiting picked up the hand-kerchief.

"Thank you, Lady Gertruda," the queen said when she had finished drinking. "Forgive me, Phoenix Dance. You see before you not only your queen but also a grieving mother. All that I have I would give to see my daughters well again. How simple a thing, to be well. We do not appreciate how sacred a thing it is when we have it. Only when it is gone do we realize how powerful a thing it is, simply to be well." The queen put the glass down; it clinked on the marble table. "I think you said there were three reasons?"

Phoenix nodded.

"May I know the other two?"

"The second reason is that I want my royal appointment back."

Queen Zandora looked puzzled.

"When you held the contest for a Shoemaker to the Royal Household," Phoenix explained, "I won. But the princesses wore out my shoes the first night, and I lost the appointment. If I discover the princesses' secret, I'd like the royal appointment back."

"And the third reason?" the queen asked.

"My great-grandmother was Her Grace, the Duchess Seagraine Dance of Trebonness. I'd like to win back the lands of my foremothers." Phoenix did not mention the fourth reason, which was that she hoped to learn something that would help her handle her illness without taking the medicine.

"Ah yes," the queen said. "I remember Seagraine from when I was a girl. What an old scamp she was. You have some of her spark and spunk, Phoenix Dance. But there is great magic at work here. It is certainly dangerous, especially if it concerns the Order of the Black Dragon. I am loathe to let my fear and grief for my own daughters put someone else's daughter at risk. Do you have your parents' permission to do this?"

"My parents are dead." On sudden impulse, Phoenix knelt beside the queen and took her hand. "Oh, please let me try!"

"Do not touch Her Majesty!" exclaimed Lady Gertruda.

"No, no, it is all right." The queen put her other hand over Phoenix's. "She is only a child. Come, tell me what is in your heart, child."

"I'm afraid for the princesses, too," Phoenix said. "When I was making their shoes, I got to know them a little. I don't want anything bad to happen to them. I want to help. Please, please let me try."

The queen sighed. "Knights, princes, and wizards have failed. Fengal, one of the most powerful wizards in the land, has failed. The king and I have both spent many nights in my daughters' room. Sometimes we look in on them every hour during the night. But we, too, have failed." She let go of Phoenix's hand and took a third handkerchief from the pile. "Perhaps you will succeed. It is certainly possible that my daughters may confide in someone their own age and sex. At this point, I am willing to try anything. Very well."

"Thank you!"

"For three nights, you may stay with my daughters in their bedchamber. They are locked in at night now, as well as having guards posted outside their doors and windows. I hate locking up my own daughters, but I don't know what else to do." She paused, drew a long sharp breath, crumpled the handkerchief in her hand, and then continued. "While you are in my household, you will be treated as an honored guest. On the third evening you are here I am hosting a masked ball to celebrate the betrothals of the eleven eldest princesses. Because you are an honored guest of the household, I will expect you to attend."

"But this is my only nice dress and it isn't—" Phoenix started to protest, but the queen held up one hand. Three gold rings flashed.

"Do not concern yourself with trifles," she said, dropping the handkerchief on the floor. "Lady Gertruda or one of my other ladies-in-waiting will find you a proper dress.

"On the morning after the third night, you will report to

me. You must have proof, however. Your word alone will not suffice. Sir Ergoth made up a fantastic story which involved elephants, believe it or not, but he offered not one shred of proof. Do you understand?"

Phoenix nodded and stood up. "When do I begin?" she asked.

"When the clock strikes ten," said the queen.

20

The First Night

PHOENIX!" AUNT LIONA EXCLAIMED IN the parlor that evening. "What in Nemaree's Name were you thinking? You should have asked us before you suggested such a crazy idea to the queen."

Aunt Mulgaussy, who was cooking dinner, waved a wooden spoon with a noodle stuck to it. "Trying to discover the princesses' secret will be dangerous. You know nothing of spells and enchantments. Seagraine knew a charm or two—love potions and such—but there's no talent for wizardry in our blood that I'm aware of."

"And your sleep will be disrupted," Aunt Twisle said. "Remember what Mederi Gale told us? If you lose sleep, you might trigger an episode of your illness, in spite of the medicine."

"You don't understand!" Phoenix sat down on the sofa with her arms crossed, her back as straight as one of Aunt Mulgaussy's knitting needles. "I want to help the princesses. And I have to get the royal appointment back. This is my one chance." She pulled on her fingers. "It's only for three days. I'll take the potion with me and take it every single night, I promise. And I'll be careful."

"The whole thing is outrageous," Aunt Liona said. "Outrageous!"

"The queen is expecting me at ten o'clock," Phoenix said. "You can't say no. You can't. You'll ruin everything!"

"What is the queen thinking?" Aunt Twisle asked. "That's what I'd like to know. She must be desperate if she's willing to send a child into danger."

"I'm not a child!" Phoenix exclaimed.

"If the queen really needs her," Aunt Mulgaussy said slowly, "it's our duty to let her go."

"Bosh!" Aunt Twisle snapped her fingers. "Surely your Royalist sympathies don't extend to sacrificing Phoenix!"

"You went behind our backs, Phoenix." Aunt Liona leaned against the curio cabinet. "I'm disappointed in you. Your uncle Horace would be disappointed in you, too."

"I'm sorry," Phoenix said. "I didn't think you would mind so much, honest! Besides, I thought you'd jump at the chance to get Trebonness back."

From the way her aunts glanced at each other, Phoenix could see they thought there wasn't much chance of this.

"I will get it back!" Phoenix struck the sofa; dust flew up. "You'll see. You've got to let me try! The queen agreed. I'm fourteen years old; I can take care of myself."

"We can only hope so," said Aunt Twisle.

Queen Zandora had told Phoenix that she expected her to live at the palace for the next three days but would permit her to go to work.

So, at ten o'clock, carrying a burlap bag containing three changes of underwear, three jars filled with her potion, a flannel nightgown, and the magic cloak the old woman had given her, Phoenix followed the queen into the princesses' bedchamber.

It was a narrow, rectangular room with a high ceiling. On one long wall, candles burned in golden heart-shaped sconces. On the other long wall, twelve arched windows, separated by white marble pillars, stood in a row. Facing each window was a bed made up with embroidered white counterpanes and white ruffled pillows. The mahogany headboards were carved with stars, moons, roses, and lilies, and each princess's name.

Phoenix followed the queen down the long room to where the princesses clustered like a flower in the middle. She passed stuffed wild animals that the taxidermist's art had made look almost real. All around the room they stood—a wolf, a cormorant, a tiger, a fox, an eagle, a swan with its wings outstretched, and the leopard that Phoenix had seen before in the princesses' parlor—all frozen in their poses, staring out with glazed glass eyes.

"Phoenix Dance," said Princess Batissa. "Look, at bedtime at least, I do not wear yellow." Like the other princesses, she wore a long-sleeved, high-necked nightgown of ivory silk with a ruched yoke across the front and ribbons at the throat and wrists.

"Hello, Princesses," Phoenix said, with a catch in her voice, so shocked was she by their appearance. In the two months since she had last seen them, they had lost weight. Their faces were as pale and sharp as though someone had stretched fine white linen over their bones. Their burning eyes shone out, restless and huge. Their necks seemed too slender to hold up their heads, and their frail fingers seemed to drip from their hands. Their anklebones, poking out from beneath their nightgowns, looked sharp and fragile, as though they would break with a single tap. Soon, Phoenix thought, the princesses would vanish altogether. They would flicker once and go out like puffs of smoke. They would surely die.

"My beloved daughters," Queen Zandora said, "Phoenix Dance will watch over you for the next three nights. I do not have to tell you why." She paused, then added, "My darlings, I ask you once again, will you not tell me what is wrong? Whatever it is, you can trust me. I only wish to help you."

The princesses merely bowed their heads and said nothing.

Queen Zandora sighed. "Well, I wish you all a good night, then. Sleep well, my dearest girls." She kissed each of them. Then, as she left, the swish of her skirts was the only sound in the room. The lock clicked behind her.

Princess Aurantica stepped forward. "Our servants have prepared a private alcove for you, Phoenix Dance. Will you please come with me?"

Phoenix followed her toward the far end of the room, passing the latest batch of new, white kid shoes lined up along the wall. As they approached the leopard and the wolf, Phoenix shivered.

"Why do you have so many . . . wild, dead animals in your room, Your Highness?" she asked. "Don't they give you nightmares?"

"Leopard used to be on display in the Great Hall," the princess said, placing her hand briefly on its head. "Where everyone stared at him all day long. It was horrible—can you imagine—to be stuffed and be put on display and then to be stared at by strangers? So I moved him to our parlor, but even there visitors stared at him. So I brought him here, where he would be free from the stares. Then, as the days went by, I rescued the other animals from various parts of the palace. They seem like friends to me now. Here is your bed."

At the end of the room, a green damask curtain screened off a narrow bed. To the right stood a potted fern, to the left, a small table made of cherrywood. Phoenix put her bag on it.

"We always drink a cup of warm wine before we go to bed," the princess said. "It helps us sleep. Please honor us by sharing a cup with us."

Phoenix hesitated. The mederi had told her to avoid drinking spirits while she was taking the potion, but Phoenix knew it would be rude to refuse the princess's offer. So she nodded. Princess Aurantica left and came back carrying a golden goblet that she handed to Phoenix. The metal felt warm and smooth against Phoenix's fingertips. She had never drunk out of any cup so fine. Steam curled up, smelling of fruit and oak. As she raised the goblet to her lips, Phoenix heard Princess Batissa call from the other side of the curtain, "Aurantica!"

"What is it?" Princess Aurantica asked, still watching Phoenix.

"I am having a premonition. Something is very wrong."

Princess Aurantica turned away at once. "What?"

"I'm not certain," said Princess Batissa, still on the other side of the curtain. "It's only a feeling. Something fluttering behind my eyes, pushing in the back of my throat."

"Well," Princess Aurantica said, "until you can tell me what is wrong, there's nothing I can do about it."

While Princess Aurantica's back was turned, Phoenix poured the wine into the potted fern. By the time Princess Aurantica finished talking with her sister and looked round again, Phoenix had the goblet to her lips with her head tipped back as though gleaning the last drops.

"Thank you." She handed back the goblet.

"Sleep well," the princess said with a slight smile, and she disappeared around the curtain.

Phoenix reached into her bag and took out one of the jars containing her potion. She unscrewed the lid and, as she had been doing for the last week, drank only a quarter of the potion. She ignored a little pang of guilt over her promise to her aunts.

As someone extinguished the candles one by one, the room grew dim; it did not turn completely black, however, so a few candles must have been left burning. Strange shadows quivered against the damask curtain. Beds creaked as the princesses slipped into them. Phoenix took off her shoes, put on her nightgown, and got into bed. It was the most comfortable bed she had ever slept in, a feather bed, with feather pillows that smelled of lavender—far different from the lumpy, musty sofa in the parlor at home. She had to fight to keep from drifting to sleep.

After perhaps half an hour, a floorboard groaned. Footsteps approached Phoenix's alcove, and the faint light brightened as someone with a candle stood over her bed. Phoenix breathed deeply and regularly, letting her eyelids flutter a little as people do when they dream. A moment later, whoever it was left.

"All is well," Princess Aurantica whispered. "The magic sleeping cup the wizard gave us worked again. She sleeps."

Magic sleeping cup! Phoenix's eyes flew open. Wizard! Had the princesses tried to cast a spell over her? Phoenix realized she could not trust them, friendly though they might seem. To them, she was an enemy. She wanted to jump up and run home. She would have given anything to be safe on her lumpy sofa, far from magic sleeping cups and treacherous princesses. She would have gladly traded her linen sheets and goose down comforter for her red quilt with its black and white diamonds.

As she lay blinking in the dim light, Phoenix heard the beds creak, then many feet padding the floor, then a moment later, the sound of weeping. It was terrible, that sound; it tore at Phoenix's heart. Tears pressed in her own eyes as she listened. Something hissed and softly slid. A click, a thud. The light of a thousand shimmering rainbows filled the air, then faded. Again the feet padded, then there was silence.

Trying to make no sound, Phoenix slipped out of bed. She peered around the curtain and almost screamed.

In the light from the three candles left burning, the shadows of the wild, dead animals flickered hugely, dancing on the walls and the beds. The leopard seemed to spring, the wolf to run, the swan to beat something with its wings. The somnolent bodies of the princesses lay in the beds, breathing softly. Twelve white cheeks rested on twelve white hands. Locks of hair fanned perfectly over pillows. Counterpanes tucked neatly under all twelve chins. All asleep. All at peace.

Phoenix drew back behind the curtain and frowned. What of the sounds she had heard? The weeping? The thud and the click? The padding feet? Something was wrong. She decided to investigate. She pulled the gray cloak out of her bag and put it on over her nightgown. After she pulled up the hood and fastened the flame-shaped clasp, she stepped around the curtain into the room. And she stood absolutely still.

Every single bed was empty. The covers were thrown back—tumbled against the footboards or hanging off the sides of the beds. The plump pillows were askew, many lying on the floor like gigantic white grubs that had come out to see the moon.

The princesses had vanished. But how? When? They had been there a moment ago. Phoenix stood, baffled, running her hand along the soft fabric of the cloak. *Sweetie dear*, she heard the old woman's words in her head. *When you wear the cloak and look out upon the world, you will see through all spells of illusion.* Phoenix clutched the flame-shaped clasp at her throat. That was it! The sight she had seen earlier of the princesses sleeping had been an illusion, an illusion intended to fool people into thinking the princesses were safe in their beds. But they *had* left when she heard their padding feet.

Then the question was, where had the princesses gone? As Phoenix tiptoed past the leopard, she noticed that the new white kid shoes were gone, too. On a small round table, the empty magic cup lay on its side and looked as though it might roll off and crash onto the floor. Phoenix approached the windows and walked beside them down the length of the room. All were shut.

At the far end of the room, where Princess Aurantica's

bed had stood, a black hole gaped in the floor. Inside, a flight of polished stone steps led downward. Voices trailed back on the currents of air gusting through the stairway— the princesses. Phoenix rolled in her lower lip, bit it, and stared down.

"Helping the princesses," she whispered, gathering her courage. "The royal appointment. Trebonness. No more potion." Then, her heart beating fast, Phoenix held her hands in front of her and stepped into the darkness.

21

The Sea Dragons

As the steps went down and down into the darkness, Phoenix pressed her hands against the tunnel walls on either side to keep from pitching forward. They felt as smooth as glass. The polished stone steps were cold against her bare feet. How had the princesses kept from slipping in their white kid shoes? Phoenix glanced back over her shoulder and saw the opening into the bedchamber as a small, gray rectangle high above. She hesitated, hugging her arms around her chest, wanting to go back, but she thought of the poor, sick princesses and went on.

After a few more minutes, the blackness faded to twilight, and after a few more steps, the stairway ended. Phoenix entered a hall lit by thick white candles burning in an iron chandelier suspended from the stone ceiling. Three arched doors opened off the hall. The sound of laughter drifted from a room on the left, where the door stood ajar. After making sure the magic cloak covered her well, Phoenix peered in and then stared in shock.

The room seemed to writhe with naked princesses. Their chaste ivory nightgowns lay scattered on chairs around the room. All they wore were their white kid shoes. Here and there, tall pillar candles burned in brass stands on the floor. A mirrored wall on one side of the room seemed to double the number of princesses.

Along the far wall stood a rack of dresses. Laughing and chattering, the princesses pulled dresses off the rack, held them against their bodies, and then looked in the mirror. Phoenix saw Princess Aurantica try two, three, then four dresses before she finally chose one made of what looked like sealskin. The skirt and bodice gleamed a shiny brown-black, with a wide band of silver scales glistening around the hem. Silver-tipped fur lined the low-plunging neckline. The sleeves billowed out from the shoulders to the elbows, where more silver scales fitted tightly down to the wrists. The dress hugged the princess's body, flaring out into a full skirt below. It was not a dress Phoenix would have expected to see on a chaste crown princess.

Phoenix slipped into the room and crouched in a corner to watch, drawing her feet well under her. No one noticed her—the cloak of invisibility seemed to be working.

Now all the other princesses were putting on equally fantastic dresses. Princess Pythia chose one made entirely of green and black snakeskin. The jet beads outlining the scaly black diamonds tinkled and swayed whenever she moved. Princess Batissa whirled in a gown covered with peacock feathers.

When all the princesses were dressed, they filed out of the room talking gaily, their cheeks red, their eyes too bright. Phoenix had never seen them so animated, not even when they were trying on their new shoes. It was as though these were completely different young women from the listless ones she knew in the palace above. Instead of being in the Kingdom of Darkness, they seemed on the edge of the Kingdom of Brilliance.

Phoenix followed the princesses back into the hall and through another arched doorway into a second tunnel. Holding a lantern high, Aurantica led them forward. Batissa went last. Phoenix followed her. The tunnel went on for a long, long way, with no turnings, no branches. When at last it began to lighten, Phoenix heard the slap of water hitting a shore. The tunnel ended. She stepped out onto a huge shelf of black rock that sloped down to the sea, which was smooth and calm. Gentle waves left necklaces of white foam on the rock. Out in the water, broken black rocks reared up like sharp teeth, stretching out as far as Phoenix could see into a silver mist that shone under a blazing full moon.

What place was this?

Phoenix looked to her left. She saw a long curve of land and, far away, the lights of her city in the center of the curve. As she stepped forward to see better, she tripped over a slab of wood. Scattered on the shore lay rotting timbers, some wide and curved, some round and long. Ropes from old rigging wound among the timbers and snaked around scattered debris: sailcloth; clothes and pots; broken lanterns, the glass gleaming in the moonlight; a sextant; a chest filled with waterlogged books; candles, tins, crates—and bones. With a sickening jolt in her stomach, Phoenix stopped, staring at the bones. Though some of the skulls were smashed in, she could see they were human. Her mouth went dry.

She knew where she was. She was on Shipwreck Point, a deserted headland of perilous rock that reached like a broken finger far out into the sea. It was said to be haunted by the ghosts of those who had drowned there. No one living ever came to this place.

What in Nemaree's Name were the princesses doing here?

Phoenix followed the princesses along the shore—placing her bare feet gingerly on the pebbles—until they reached a dock thrusting into the water. Its wooden pilings were carved with fish; each had a grotesque human face.

Princess Aurantica picked up a conch shell from the edge of the dock, raised it to her lips, and blew. The roar of sound echoed off the rock. A few moments later, all across the surface of the sea, luminous white bubbles frothed, shimmering, arching, swirling into whirlpools. Next, little waves sploshed and played, then bigger waves rolled back and forth. A pale green loop like the coil of a gigantic snake broke the water's surface. Then another loop rose and another, coil after coil until at last a monstrous head reared up with water dripping from its long pointed snout.

Phoenix stepped back, clutching her hands to her chest.

Attached to the coils, enormous fins swept up and down—or were they wings? Emerald green, fluted like scallop shells, the winglike fins were almost transparent, the undersides gleaming like mother-of-pearl. More coils appeared around the monster, looping and looping until there seemed to be hundreds. Phoenix wondered if she were seeing Galgantica. Then more heads broke the surface, and as the great creatures towered up, gliding on the water, Phoenix realized they were sea dragons—though they were much different from the one in Sea Dragon Fountain. That one was like a lizard with wings; these were like crosses between a sea serpent and a dragon, with the winglike fins sprouting from five places along each sinuous, looping body.

In spite of their size, the sea dragons looked surprisingly delicate, tinted pale pink, green, and blue, shining as though made of blown glass. Brilliant silver eyes sat on either side of their long, graceful heads, which they swung from side to side. In the middle of each monster's forehead, a glowing golden horn shone.

Phoenix drew the magic cloak close around her, whispering over and over, "They cannot see me, they cannot see me."

When the sea dragon nearest the dock opened its mouth and bellowed—a low musical sound—a row of sharp teeth glistened. One long wisp of fire curled out of its throat and danced into the air. In spite of the magic cloak, Phoenix was about to run back to the safety of the tunnel when she saw the princesses, unafraid, walk to the water's edge.

Not far out, bobbing amid the sea dragons, strange creatures swam—creatures with the tails of fish and the torsos and heads of men. Phoenix guessed they were mermen: the children of Nemaree and Saducus, a mortal hero from the dawn of Windward. She had heard them described in tales and old songs.

One of these mermen swam toward the shore, his tail flashing. Princess Aurantica threw him the conch shell, which he raised to his lips and blew. Again, the blast echoed off the rock. This time, flurries of blue light sparkled out of the conch shell and whisked and spun over the merman. A moment later, with water dripping down his body, he rose from a crouch and walked on two legs up onto the shore.

Phoenix stood, transfixed.

Mighty muscles covered the merman's chest, arms, and stomach. Around his neck, a necklace of orange coral and shark's teeth clinked as he walked. Below, he wore tights lined with iridescent silvery green fish scales. His feet were bare. He bowed to Princess Aurantica, then tossed the conch shell to another merman waiting in the water, who raised it to his lips and blew. He, too, was transformed by flurries of blue light, and he, too, walked onto the shore. This process continued until three dozen mermen stood before the princesses.

Princess Aurantica stepped forward. "My sisters," she said in a loud, joyful voice, "let the choosing begin!"

One by one, in order of age, each princess walked up to a different merman and held out her hand. Each merman who was chosen removed a crown of woven kelp, seaweed, and barnacles from his head and placed it on the head of his princess. Those mermen not chosen dove into the water, where their legs melded back into tails.

Even wrapped in her cloak of invisibility, Phoenix shivered, watching the mermen, watching the sea dragons glide on the sea, which lolled like a huge black tongue. A strange wind blew, smelling of sweat and soot. Whelk, Aunt Mulgaussy, and the queen had been right. There was magic here, great magic. How could Phoenix possibly hope to break this spell? What was the spell?

Princess Aurantica and her merman walked out onto the dock. A sapphire blue sea dragon, one of the largest, glided over to the dock and reared up higher and higher into the air. The horn sticking out of its forehead flashed—sharp, dangerous, wicked. Phoenix put her hand to her mouth to keep from crying out.

Then Princess Aurantica raised her arms high overhead, as though in invocation, and she curtsied to the sea dragon.

There was an explosion of orange light—a flash, a boom—and the monster transformed into a glass gondola with the head of a sea dragon. The winglike fins, inscribed in glass, were folded back along the sides of the boat. Only the horn, shining with a radiant golden light, seemed still alive. The princess and the merman stepped in, and the merman rowed the gondola out into the sea.

One by one, all of the other princesses did as Princess Aurantica had done. When, last of all, Princess Batissa was climbing into her gondola, Phoenix knew she should sneak in beside her, but Phoenix's feet would not move. What if the boat turned back into a sea dragon in the middle of the ocean? Who were these handsome mermen, and why did the princesses trust them? Where were they going? How could riding in a gondola wear out the princesses' shoes? So many questions needed answers. However, no matter how hard Phoenix thought of all her reasons for discovering the princesses' secret, she could not bring herself to set foot in a sea dragon gondola.

When all the gondolas were out of sight on the far side of the black rocks, and she could no longer see even the shining horns, Phoenix turned to go back to the tunnel. Then, out of the corner of her eye, she saw something glimmering on the rock near the edge of the dock. She walked over and picked up a cluster of scales that had fallen from one of the mermen's tights. They looked like fish scales, but they were made of soft, pliable silver and rippled with an iridescent blue light. Remembering that the queen wanted proof, Phoenix slipped them into her pocket.

She walked back to the tunnel. She made her way in the darkness to the hall with the iron chandelier, up the long, slippery stairway, and past the shadows of the wild animals flickering over the princesses' rumpled beds. She crawled into her feather bed. In spite of its comfort and its lavender-scented pillows, Phoenix slept little that night. Her mind was in a fever, going over all she had seen.

Near dawn, Phoenix felt a rush of wind coming up the stairway, smelled the salty tang of seaweed and sweat mixed with the scent of soot, and then heard the patter of feet as the princesses returned. She did not have to look to know that the white kid shoes were worn to tatters.

22

The Second Night

T HAT'S A PRETTY TALL TALE, PHOENIX," Whelk said after work the next day. They were walking along Harbor Road, north of the market. Above them, seagulls circled and wailed.

Phoenix watched them. She had slipped out of the palace after the princesses had fallen asleep.

She was not tired at all but keyed up from the night's adventure and from not taking all her potion. Though she had not wanted to go to Whelk for help, she did not know whom else to ask about the magic she had witnessed the night before.

"It's true," she said, surprised he did not believe her. "Every word."

"Oh, come now." He laughed. "Mermen? Sea dragons

that turn into glass gondolas? I don't want to call you a liar, but maybe the potion has affected your senses."

"I have proof." Phoenix reached into her skirt pocket and pulled out the cluster of silver scales that had dropped from one of the mermen's tights. Even though the clouds swirled as thick as clotted cream in the sky, the scales still glistened with an iridescent blue light. She handed the cluster to Whelk.

He ran his forefinger over the scales, prodding them. They gave slightly, but as soon as he removed his finger, the impression sprang back. Blue light clung to his finger for a moment, circling it, then vanished.

"Well," he said, "I have to admit, I've never seen anything like this. It does look magical." He frowned, the skin at the top of his nose rumpling against his forehead. "Do you swear on the song of the Sea Maid that you're telling the truth?"

"I swear on the song of the Sea Maid, on the heart of Nemaree, and on the treasure of Kloud. It all happened just as I told you. Tomorrow I can bring the magic cloak to show you if you want."

Whelk nodded, and his face lit up. "If it's true, this is fabulous magic. I knew the princesses were under some kind of spell, but this! This is incredible. Kloud's Bounty! I wish I were a wizard."

"Me too." Phoenix sighed. "Then you could tell me how to break the spell, whatever it is. I have two more nights to figure it all out."

"You've got to sneak aboard one of those gondolas and find out where the princesses are going. It's the only way."

"But I'm scared. What if the gondolas turn back into sea dragons in the middle of the sea?"

Whelk shook his head. "Not likely. After all, the princesses come back each night."

"That's true enough."

"I'll go to the Book Tower right now and see if I can find out anything about sea dragons."

They parted. Phoenix headed for the palace.

That night, everything happened almost the same as it had the night before. Again Princess Aurantica brought Phoenix the magic sleeping cup; again Princess Batissa caused a distraction with an even more vigorous premonition of doom; again Phoenix poured the wine into the potted fern; and again she drank only a quarter of her potion. After the princesses went down the stairway, Phoenix followed in the magic cloak, wearing her shoes this time. The princesses chose different dresses and different mermen from the night before. When Princess Batissa stepped into the sea dragon gondola, Phoenix stood poised behind her on the dock.

Phoenix sagged beneath the magic cloak, wanting to go back, to go home, to go anywhere else, but she thought of the princesses and strengthened her resolve. She had to save them if she could, had to find a way to break the spell they were under. After taking a deep breath, she reached out one foot, then stepped into the gondola. It dipped.

"What was that!" Princess Batissa exclaimed.

The merman seemed to look straight at Phoenix. Since he was a magical being himself, she feared he might be able to see through the cloak of invisibility.

"It was nothing, Princess," he said. "Only a wave."

Phoenix nearly sighed with relief but caught herself in time to keep from making a sound. She sat behind the princess and watched the merman row the gondola. His curling blond locks caressed his shoulders. A necklace of spotted cowrie shells hung over the muscles on his bare chest, which gleamed and rippled as he rowed. When he lifted the oar, the water dripped off the tip in a silver stream. She thought of Whelk, wondered what he would look like without his shirt, and then blushed at having such thoughts.

They wound their way between the towering black rocks, which loomed up like sentinels one after the other, their edges sharp, their shadows deep. Sometimes the passage between two rocks was so narrow that if Phoenix had stretched out her arms, her fingers would have swept the rock on either side. The sea was unnaturally calm, the water black as coal. The horn on the glass sea dragon shone with a soft, steady light, leading the way, but the light did not reach far into the darkness.

On and on they went until the rocks, growing smaller and farther apart, at last ended with one final ragged stump. As the twelve gondolas spread out upon the sea, the shining horns bobbed across the water, scattered like diamonds thrown onto a black velvet cloth. Phoenix craned her head all around, but she could not see beyond the mist that wreathed all sides of the horizon.

A few minutes later, they entered the mist. Cold tiny droplets clung to Phoenix's face, and she shivered. She heard music, faint at first, then growing louder and louder. Drums, tambouras, and pipes; lutes and viols and crashing cymbals were led by a wild sweet voice soaring up like a fountain. The voice was not quite human. There seemed to be a howling note to it, a baying, a wildness that ripped at her heart and at something deeper—some older, rapacious part of her mind. Some of the words were Archipelagan, but most were not. Phoenix leaned forward, eager to hear more.

"Hurry," said Princess Batissa to her merman. "The flame sings!"

The gondola slid against something—the side of a ship; its masts and sails lost in the silvery mist. A rope ladder hung down over the side.

"I am the youngest and always last," Princess Batissa said and sighed. Then she and her merman climbed up. Phoenix followed.

As soon as she stepped onto the ship, Phoenix darted behind a stack of barrels piled on the deck. She could just see the edges of the purple sails before they vanished into the mist. Soon, the deck began to rise and fall. When a gust of wind blew past, Phoenix smelled smoke.

A glow of light came from the direction of the bow. Phoenix crept around the barrels and ran perhaps twenty feet toward the bow, crouching down again behind a coil of rope. She peered around the rope, and what she saw was so beautiful and strange that she raised her hands to her cheeks.

On the deck, beneath a row of hanging lanterns, the twelve princesses danced with their mermen. Beyond them on the prow rose the figurehead of the ship, a great dragon cast in black metal that leaned out over the water. A flame roared from its open mouth, surging two, three, then four feet into the air. The princesses faced this flame as they danced. The white ermine trim on Princess Osea's dress took on a reddish sheen from the flame.

The flickering light slid over the princesses' curving arms and over the black dragon's curving wings. The princesses followed no set dance steps that Phoenix could see, but each moved in her own way. They stomped their feet, then whirled and leaped and shimmied to the rhythm of the drums. Gourds rattled and thrummed. Pipes wailed. The wild, sweet inhuman voice sang on.

Moving among the dancers, dancing with first one princess, then another, was a tall masked man in a black cloak that flared and rippled, revealing a scarlet lining which shone like the red flame in the dragon's mouth. The cloak brushed against the princesses' skirts, billowed out, then touched the ship's railing, always moving, a devouring shadow, a black and red wave.

As Phoenix watched and listened, her feet began to move. She forgot about saving the princesses. She forgot about breaking the spell. Without knowing what she was doing, drawn, compelled, her heart pulled like a moth toward the black dragon's flame, she ran around the coil of rope and joined the princesses dancing before the black dragon. Her legs began to jump, her arms raised over her head, her body bent and twirled.

"Yip—ye-ye-ye-ye!" Princess Aurantica shouted. The other princesses shouted back. Princess Aurantica's merman picked her up and swung her in a circle. The sleeve on her dress slipped down, exposing her shoulder.

Time passed. Phoenix sprang into the air again and again, lifted by the flame, the flame, always the flame, until she was burning inside. The flame sang only to her, only of her. It saw past the magic cloak, past her nightgown, past her skin and bones into her soul itself. It sang of everything she longed for, hoped for, everything she dreamed of and might become. She was alive! Alive! She had left the great gray plain behind. She wanted more and more!

The masked man in the whirling black cloak moved toward her, three princesses away, then two, then one. He cannot see me, Phoenix thought, her heart beating wildly, he cannot see me. But then he was reaching for her, looming above her, and his hands seized hers.

23

The Black Wizard

PHOENIX AND THE MAN DANCED, HALF surrounded by the whirling black cloak with its red lining. The black mask the man wore was shaped like a dragon's head. Shining scales glittered across the front, with wings folded back along the sides. On one of his fingers shone a gold ring shaped like a dragon; a red ruby sparkled in its mouth. With one hand he unfastened the clasp on Phoenix's magic cloak, tore it off, and tossed it onto the deck.

"Who have we here?" he asked, spinning her around.

Phoenix did not speak. Her mouth was dry, her throat like sandpaper. Then she felt compelled to speak.

"I am Phoenix Dance. I followed the princesses here from the palace."

"I see," he said. "So the magic cup and sleeping illusion failed at last. Vanquished by a mere girl in a magic cloak."

But Phoenix didn't care about any of that. Her mind was fixed on only one thing.

"The flame," she said, reaching toward it. "It's so beautiful. What makes it burn?"

"Inside the metal dragon, behind the crystal window, is the living heart of a black dragon. The flame draws its power from that."

Black dragon? Phoenix shivered, her head suddenly clear. "You're one of those evil wizards from the Order of the Black Dragon! Why did you cast this terrible spell? Why do the princesses want only to dance before this flame—and me, too? How come nothing else matters?"

"Because as the princesses dance before the flame, they are more alive than they have ever been before. They live more in each moment than they have lived in all their lives."

Phoenix thought how, even during the day, when the princesses were not dancing, they longed for the flame, the music, and the dance, and how all of this longing was focused into an obsession over their shoes.

"But why?" Phoenix asked. "Why did you do this?"

"For power, my dear. The one thing any wizard wants more of. As the princesses dance, their intense feelings feed the black dragon's flame, and the flame feeds me."

Phoenix looked at Princess Aurantica dancing with her merman. She learned backward, her fragile arms reaching toward the mist that veiled the ship like a wraith; her hands bent so that a red spot reflected from the flame appeared on each thin wrist. Soon she would be a wraith herself.

"But the princesses are so weak," Phoenix said to the black wizard. "Soon they will die!"

He laughed. "That has its uses, too. Now, the question is, what are we to do with you? You know the secret. I would turn you into a scuttling spider for your snooping, but you look so much like someone I once knew, someone dear to me. Who was your mother?"

"Aviel Dance."

The masked wizard nodded. "Yes, the resemblance is uncanny. The slant of the eyes, the line of the jaw . . ." He reached out and drew one finger along Phoenix's cheek. She shuddered.

"I must think what is to be done with you," he said. "Meanwhile, dance! I will not gain as much power from you as from them, for they have royal blood. But I will get some. Dance!"

He went to the next princess, and Phoenix started dancing wildly. She did not want to stop, in spite of what the black wizard had told her. She felt as alive as she did in the Kingdom of Brilliance, alive and on fire, dazzling. Blisters rose on her feet where her shoes chafed her, but she did not care because the pain only made her feel more alive.

Not until hours had passed—or was it a moment?—did the black wizard suddenly raise one hand toward the flame. An arc of red light flashed between the flame on the black dragon and the ruby ring on the wizard's finger. Then the flame dropped low. With a long sharp shrill note, the music ceased. Phoenix felt the deck of the ship stop rising and falling. Three of the princesses fell to their knees.

"The flame!" Princess Aurantica cried. "Turn up the flame! Let us dance, oh, please, I beg you, let us dance!"

"Tomorrow night," said the masked wizard. Then he turned to Phoenix.

"I will lay a binding spell upon you," he said, "so that you cannot speak of this to anyone." He laid both hands on Phoenix's head and spoke some magic words. Then he walked toward the princesses. While his back was turned, Phoenix grabbed the magic cloak, wadded it up, and stuffed it under her arm.

"Now, Princesses," the black wizard said, "I command you, return to your gondolas."

Listless, some of them weeping, the princesses climbed down the rope ladder with their mermen into the sea dragon gondolas. Phoenix climbed into the boat with Princess Batissa, who was sobbing and did not seem to notice her.

The mermen rowed them back through the mist, back between the treacherous rocks to the dock. Slowly, slowly, the princesses made their way through the long tunnel to the wardrobe room, where they changed back into their nightgowns. Then they climbed the stairs to their bedchamber. There, as the guttering candles flickered against the walls, the princesses surrounded Phoenix.

"We should throw her in the dungeon for spying upon us!" exclaimed Princess Batissa.

"Hush, Batissa!" Princess Aurantica said; then she turned

to Phoenix. "Are you going to tell our mother the queen what you have learned?"

"I must try. In spite of the binding spell."

"Please do not," Princess Aurantica said. "We beg you. When we are dancing we are more alive than we have ever been. We choose our partners. We do not want to give that up."

"But it's destroying you," Phoenix said. "Don't you want to be well?"

"You must give us one more night," Princess Aurantica pleaded. "Just one more night. My mother gave you three nights with us. Please, let us have one more night."

Phoenix looked at them standing there so thin and pale and desperate, so ill. The princesses seemed hollow, like delicate snail shells one could hold to one's ear and hear a dim roaring from the emptiness within. Phoenix felt raw inside herself, as though something had been scraped out of her. She could see how if this dancing went on night after night, she would turn into a hollow shell, too.

And yet she could not refuse the princesses' request. Not because they begged her. Not because she wanted to find a way to break the masked wizard's spell. But because more than anything else Phoenix wanted to dance before the black dragon's flame on the enchanted ship again. Could one last night of dancing really hurt the princesses any more than they were already hurt? Phoenix clasped her hands, feeling a little guilty. If she did what was best for the princesses, she would rush down the ornate hallways, find the queen, and try to tell her everything this instant. But the black dragon's flame burned in front of her eyes, the intoxicating flame.

"Well?" asked Princess Osea. "Will you give us one more night?"

"All right," Phoenix said. "One more night. Then I must find a way to tell the queen—in spite of the wizard's binding spell. And I'm going with you to dance again."

All the princesses nodded, but Phoenix saw a strange look pass between Princess Osea and Princess Aurantica.

After breakfast at the palace—sausage, toast, stewed plums, and three kinds of eggs—Phoenix went straight to work. She was too riled up by the wild dancing and the events of the past night to sleep. She felt full of zest, on the threshold of the Kingdom of Brilliance. To her delight, she had left the great gray plain behind. Her plan to take only a quarter of the potion had worked. Now if she could just stay on the threshold and not plunge into the frenzied heart of the Kingdom of Brilliance . . .

"Did you sneak into one of the gondolas?" Whelk asked her in a whisper when she came in.

Phoenix tried to say yes and could not. The binding spell. "Let's talk at lunch," she said.

When lunchtime came, Whelk suggested they go into the alley, where they could speak privately.

When the door closed behind them, Phoenix said, "A binding spell has been laid upon me so I can't talk about what happened."

"Let me see if I can break it," Whelk said. He chanted words over her. "Try now."

She opened her mouth and tried to tell him about the enchanted dragon ship, but her tongue seemed to be held down by a brick. She shook her head.

"It's not working," she whispered.

"I just don't have enough power to break the spell," Whelk said. "There's got to be another way." He stroked the carving of Galgantica hanging around his neck. He bit his thumbnail. He tapped his toe. At last he said, "I know. I'll just slip inside the spell. Try to put a little kink in it so you can write about what happened. Stay here a moment."

He hurried into the shop and returned with paper, an inkpot, and a quill. Back in the alley, he spoke more magic words. Then Phoenix laid the paper against a cobblestone and tried to write, but her fingers would not move. Ink dripped off the tip of the quill and made a chicken-shaped blot on the paper.

Whelk frowned. "Maybe if I say my spell backward— sometimes that works."

This time Phoenix found that her fingers moved, and the words flowed out of the quill. She scribbled down all that had happened with the princesses and the masked wizard.

"Incredible!" Whelk exclaimed, reading over her shoulder as she wrote. "I wish I could see that! And I'd sure love to borrow that magic cloak, so I could study how it works."

So how do I break the masked wizard's spell over the princesses? Phoenix wrote at the end.

Whelk looked thoughtful. "The dragon's flame is the key. The masked wizard draws his power from the dragon's heart, which creates the flame. The answer is simple. To break the spell you have to put out the flame."

Phoenix felt a jump of alarm inside her. The flame was so beautiful; she hated the thought of putting it out.

But how would I do it? Pour water on it? It would be awfully hard to climb up on the dragon with a bucket of water. Especially as it leans out so far over the sea.

"Let me think," Whelk said. As he did, Phoenix stared at his face, at the cleft in his chin, at the circles of gold surrounding the blue irises in his eyes. How she had missed him. A small, soft spot in her heart ached as though someone were pressing a spoon against it. It felt wonderful to be talking with him again, wonderful to have him all to herself.

"What we need is sand," Whelk said. "Enchanted sand that you can pour into the black dragon's mouth. If you can get the sand—it won't take much, perhaps two cupfuls—I think I can enchant it."

"Why not ask your uncle Fengal to help us?" Phoenix asked. "Surely he's powerful enough to defeat the masked wizard."

"He's away on some business with the High Council of Wizards. So I'm afraid you're on your own." He drew his eyebrows together. "You'll be all right. Won't you?"

Phoenix picked up the piece of paper she had written on and slowly crumpled it. "I don't know. But I have to try to help the princesses." She paused. "Why do *you* want to help them?" she asked. "After what the queen did to your father . . ."

Whelk stiffened. "He was a bad man. I'm nothing like him. That's why I want to help the princesses. To prove I'm nothing like him. I take after my uncle."

Phoenix nodded, then turned to go back into the shop. But Whelk grabbed her arm.

"Wait, Phoenix! There's something else you should know. Something I once read about black dragons."

"What?"

"It is said that if you touch the heart of a black dragon, you'll be cured of any illness."

She stared at him. "Any illness?"

"Yes."

Phoenix felt something leap inside her. For a moment everything turned yellow, as though she were seeing through a blaze of sunlight. There was a cure for the Illness of the Two Kingdoms? A cure! She could be well? Without the medicine?

But how? How could she touch the black dragon's heart?

There was a crystal window in the metal dragon, she remembered. She could see the heart glowing through it. If she could break the window, she could touch the heart. She pressed her fingertips together as though in prayer. "I would be cured," she whispered. But a funny, fluttery, uncertain feeling pushed up from her stomach into her throat.

After lunch, Phoenix could not settle into anything. She started attaching a sole to a boot, stopped, started sewing the parts of a green silk shoe together, stopped, and then started organizing the ribbons on the ribbon rack. But she left that half finished, too. She whistled as she darted about.

"Phoenix!" Percy Snailkips exclaimed. "Corns and bunions! What's wrong with you today?"

"I was up most of the night," she said. But she knew that was only part of her problem. What was wrong with her was that she had been taking only a quarter of her potion and she was becoming "flighty," as her Aunt Mulgaussy would say.

"Come with me to the alley," Percy Snailkips said.

She followed him outside.

"I didn't want to say this in front of the others," the shoemaker began, "but I've been watching your work for some time now. And I have to say, I'm not satisfied. You're distracted half the time, it seems, and don't finish up your tasks. Or you talk up a storm, wasting the day. You've another two weeks until your probation is finished. And I'm sorry to say that if you don't show a big improvement, I'm going to have to let you go."

"Let me go!" Phoenix gasped. "But I love shoemaking!"

"I'm sorry. My mind's made up. You've got two weeks to convince me otherwise. Take the rest of the afternoon off to think over what I've said." And he went back inside the shop.

Phoenix stood blinking back tears, her arms pressed tight against her body. This could not be happening. What would she do?

24

Fighting

PHOENIX LEFT THE SHOEMAKER'S SHOP and walked through the city, hardly knowing where she was going. A drizzling rain fell. She did not bother to pull up her hood, and soon her hair was sodden. Only one thought filled her mind: how could she convince Percy Snailkips to let her keep her job? *Take the potion,* a voice whispered inside her. *Take it all.* But if everything went well, after she touched the black dragon's heart tonight, she would never have to take the potion again. She had stolen a hammer from the shop to break the crystal window. It hung beneath her petticoat, fastened with a length of string.

However, as she felt its weight along her leg, the funny, fluttery feeling rose into her throat again. It beat there like a trapped dove until at last she understood what it was telling her. If she was cured of her illness, she would never experience the Kingdom of Brilliance again. She would lose that wonderful feeling forever. But Phoenix knew, deep in her heart, that she could not have the Kingdom of Brilliance without the Kingdom of Darkness. And she hated that dark, awful place.

She went to the palace, to the princesses' bedchamber. Luckily, they were not there. Phoenix dug the magic cloak out of her bag—still on the cherrywood table beside her feather bed—and stroked the soft gray wool, reluctant to part with it. But the cloak had served its purpose; besides, she was only loaning it to Whelk. She bundled it beneath her arm and left the palace.

On Harbor Road she paid a shellnar for a cloth bag. Down at the sandy beach near the south end of the road, she scooped two cupfuls of sand into the bag and knotted it off with string. Then she started back toward the shop, her mind so full of the evening ahead—jitters over the princesses' Betrothal Ball, delight over the prospect of dancing before the black dragon's flame, fear over trying to smother the flame without the masked wizard killing her— that she barely noticed where she was going and made several wrong turns.

When she became aware of her surroundings again, Phoenix found herself standing outside the shabby graystone building that the Archipelago Party rented for its activities. Three cracked steps led up to the oak door. An ache filled her chest. Rora. She wanted Rora. Some part of her had known that and led her here.

The door creaked as Phoenix went in. No one was inside. Freshly printed pamphlets waiting to be folded covered four long plank tables. Then she heard the clang of metal against metal and someone cursing.

"Stoven and sunk! Why won't this thing work!" It was Rora's voice, coming from around a partition in the back. Phoenix's heart leaped. She hurried down the room and stepped around the partition, but she saw only a monstrous black printing press. When Phoenix walked around the printing press, she saw Rora crouched behind it with a wrench in her hand. Pieces of black metal lay scattered on the floor. A smudge of grease smeared her left cheek.

"Rora?" she said.

Rora looked up. "Yes? Oh, it's *you*."

"What are you doing?"

"Trying to fix this blasted thing. I took it apart, but now I can't put it together again."

Phoenix knelt beside her, put down the magic cloak and the little bag of sand, then picked up one of the pieces—a long metal bar. After turning it in her hand, she studied the printing press.

"It looks like this piece goes here," she said, and she fit it between two slots.

Rora stared.

"I have to talk to you, Rora," Phoenix said. "I can't stand this fight we're in. Besides, I need your advice. Please let me tell you what happened that night in Parliament Square. I have to. I just have to."

Rora did not look at her but traced one hand along the wheel on the printing press. "All right. I'm listening. Talk."

"I didn't turn the guards on you. Honest. I ran around the corner of the building and was hiding behind the rhododendron bushes when the guards ran by me. I had my cheek pressed up against the side of the building. It was very cold and rough. It was a cold night, wasn't it? I was so scared, I didn't know what to do. I was still holding the paintbrush. I saw the guards grab you—"

"What! You saw them grab me? And you didn't try to help me?"

"But there were four of them, Rora. What could I have done?"

Rora hit the printing press with the wrench. It rang. "You shouldn't have abandoned me! We could have gone to prison together. Then I wouldn't have suffered alone." She clutched the wrench to her chest. "I will never, ever forgive you for that."

Phoenix felt as though a hand were squeezing her heart. "But, Rora, I need your help! I need to talk to you about the princesses and their secret—"

"Fie on the princesses!"

"Only not just about them, but about Whelk, and the potion, and, oh, Rora, I know you don't like Percy Snailkips, but I might lose my job and—"

"I don't care. Do you hear me? I don't care one little bit. I saw what you did at the demonstration a few weeks ago. You left right in the middle! How could you? Well, for your information we actually have a meeting with ten important Members of Parliament. They were so impressed by our courage and our peaceful demonstration that they agreed to hear our demands—no, not demands, Elior said to call them suggestions." A puzzled look crossed Rora's face. "All this time I've been fighting the wrong way—"

She stopped and scowled at Phoenix. "But you, you wouldn't know the first thing about courage, or about fighting for something you believe in. You're a coward."

A hot spike seemed to drive into the top of Phoenix's head and thrust through her body. She seized the metal bar that she had inserted into the printing press, ripped it out, and flung it across the room.

25

The Betrothal Ball

THAT EVENING WAS THE BETROTHAL Ball, which the queen had commanded Phoenix to attend. She stood in her borrowed blue silk dress, half hidden behind a potted tree in the palace ballroom. The silk felt like the brush of feathers against her shoulders and arms. Phoenix began to imagine what Rora would say if she saw her wearing such an expensive dress, then caught herself and shrugged. She no longer cared what Rora thought of her, not anymore, not after the cruel things Rora had said.

After their fight, Phoenix had stormed out of the building and taken the magic cloak and the little bag of sand to Whelk. Muttering and sweating, he had at last enchanted the sand—she hoped. He had said there was no way to know whether the spell worked until she poured it down the black dragon's throat. And how, she wondered, touching the pink velvet rose pinned to her waist, would she do that without the masked wizard seeing her?

Phoenix looked around the ballroom, praying no one would ask her to dance. The walls were painted with scenes from Windward's history: the birth of the archipelago, when Nemaree sang the islands from the sea; the battle of Kloud and Contumi for rule of the skies; and the rise of the House of Seaborne a thousand years ago—when the magic white sword with the blue sea-stone in the hilt had been wielded by the first queen, Coranna of Noralinden. Above, hanging from the ceiling, illuminating the paintings as well as the men and women in their silks and satins, a row of crystal chandeliers blazed. Their droplets of light spattered over the princesses, who were lined up in a row from eldest to youngest, waiting to be asked to dance.

Except for Princess Aurantica, dressed in gray as usual, the princesses wore demure pastel-colored dresses—Princess Batissa in a yellow silk so pale it was almost ivory. Flesh-colored masks covered their eyes and foreheads, leaving their mouths exposed so everyone could see they never smiled. Not once. The masks were all the same shape—curving inward on the sides and pointed at the corners—so the princesses looked as though dead butterflies had been pinned on their faces. They made Phoenix want to weep. For a moment, thinking of how Rora had smashed the statues, Phoenix had the wild idea that the princesses wore the masks to hide their ruined faces. No one else wore a mask.

"On display again, aren't they?" said a woman's voice.

Phoenix turned. Behind her, wearing a gown of dark green brocade, stood the Nautilus. The braided and curled mass of red hair piled on her head made her seem even taller than usual. Around her throat was a collar studded with emeralds. A diamond bracelet sparkled on her wrist. Her shoes were hidden by her dress.

"Hello, my lady," Phoenix said.

"You must be Phoenix Dance, the young woman who dares to try to learn the princesses' secret," said the Nautilus.

"Yes, my lady." Phoenix was amazed that the proud and haughty Nautilus had deigned to speak to her.

"I imagine this is the first time a shoemaker's apprentice has ever been invited to a royal ball."

"Probably, my lady."

"Is it true that you are a fabulous shoemaker?"

"Not yet. But someday I will make the most beautiful shoes in the kingdom."

The Nautilus laughed. "You remind me of myself when I was your age. When you are finished with the princesses, come to me and make me a pair of dancing slippers. I will pursue anything that will continue to make me the most beautiful dancer in the kingdom."

"As you wish, my lady," Phoenix said, and she turned back to watch the princesses. A man wearing a blue sash studded with medals had walked up to Princess Aurantica and appeared to be asking her to dance. He was neither fat nor thin, handsome nor plain. He had brown hair, a clipped mustache, and looked neither young nor old.

"Do you know who he is?" Phoenix asked the Nautilus.

"Her betrothed. The good and worthy Lord Halisor of Winsette. Our future consort king."

"But she doesn't even smile at him."

"Why should she? Aurantica did not choose him. The queen did. Aurantica had no say in the matter of whom she would spend her life with. Nor did any of the other princesses whose betrothals we are 'celebrating.'" The Nautilus lowered her voice. "No wonder Aurantica has worn nothing but gray since the day her betrothal was arranged."

Now all twelve princesses had been led out onto the dance floor. The men lined up on one side, the princesses across from them. The harps, viols, and lutes played a stately, measured tune, and the sedate dance began. Gloved hands reached for gloved hands. All the dancers moved in exactly the same patterns of steps, the men and women mirror images of each other. The princesses did not smile or talk.

"Once," the Nautilus said, "my mother tried to arrange my life for me, until I stopped her by desecrating the Sea Maid's holy temple."

"You what!" Phoenix gasped.

"Let the princesses keep their secret, I say. If it brings them any joy and freedom. Any life of their own."

Phoenix watched Princess Aurantica, so thin and so pale, move stiffly around the ballroom opposite Lord Halisor.

"But look at them," Phoenix said to the Nautilus. "They're so thin. They're slowly wasting away. They're in the

Nethersea, the Kingdom of Darkness, by day at least. What kind of life is that?"

"Perhaps it is the price they pay for the secret life they have at night, when they wear out their shoes. Sometimes we pay a high price for passion and power. Often, after I have given a performance that I have poured myself into, I am only a rag, nothing, an empty cup."

However, as Phoenix watched the princesses dancing, their masked faces cold and dead, her heart filled with pity, her mind with doubt. Was the Kingdom of Brilliance worth the Kingdom of Darkness? For her and for them?

After the ball, when the princesses and Phoenix returned to their bedchamber at midnight, the princesses dropped onto their beds with their shoulders slumped, obviously exhausted. Phoenix feared they would not go to the enchanted dragon ship, and she would lose her last opportunity—for this was her third and final night—to break the spell and cure her illness. About curing her illness, though, she still felt ambivalent.

However, Phoenix was taking no chances. She ducked behind the damask curtain that screened her bed and tied the hammer and little bag of enchanted sand under her petticoat. It was a good thing she did, too, because when she came out again, Princess Aurantica had walked to the marble pillar that separated the two arched windows in front of her bed. She leaned her cheek against the pillar and began to weep, letting her tears roll down the marble.

Phoenix wanted to weep herself when she saw how easily Princess Aurantica's grief flowed. When the princess's tears trailed into a crack in the marble, with a slight creak her bed sank into the floor. As the hole with the stairway opened wide, a flood of light shot out of it and whisked through the room, sparkling in every color of the rainbow. Phoenix closed her eyes against the brightness. When she opened them, she saw that all the princesses were sleeping soundly in their beds. But they were also standing beside her!

The princesses laughed at her astonished face.

"When the secret stairway opens, it triggers the spell of illusion," Princess Natica explained. "The illusion also keeps anyone from seeing the stairway."

Phoenix reached over and touched the illusion of the sleeping Princess Batissa. Her hand felt warm flesh.

"But her arm feels real!" Phoenix exclaimed.

"The masked wizard is a powerful spell-master," Princess Osea said.

"Come," said Princess Aurantica, "let us go. It is late, and we are wasting precious time."

One by one, Princess Aurantica leading with the lantern, the princesses filed down the stairs. Phoenix went last.

When they reached the wardrobe chamber, the princesses insisted that Phoenix choose a dress for herself. They crowded around her, holding up dress after dress, except for Princess Aurantica, who watched from a distance, her face dispassionate. Protesting but secretly delighted, Phoenix chose a dress of different shades of red: red-orange sleeves made of fish scales, a bodice stitched with red feathers, a magenta belt, and cranberry sequins scattered across the scarlet netting of the skirt. Over the dress she wore a cloak of the lightest silk in a shade of red so dark it was almost black.

"Why does the masked wizard provide you with dresses but not shoes?" Phoenix asked.

"He would take pleasure in seeing us dance barefoot," said Princess Osea.

"But we refuse him in this," Princess Aurantica said. "We have our dignity."

Phoenix followed the princesses through the arched double doors and into the long tunnel. On and on they went until at last they emerged at Shipwreck Point to the sound of waves beating against the shore. The night was cold. After the princesses had chosen their mermen and the sea dragons began to surface, Princess Aurantica turned to Phoenix and said, "Tonight you will ride in my gondola."

Together they walked onto the dock; Phoenix's heart beat fast as a green and gold sea dragon approached, its head held high on its sinuous neck, its winglike fins sweeping up and down. A jet of fire streaked from its mouth. After Princess Aurantica bowed low, the sea dragon transformed into a glass gondola with a glowing horn, and they stepped inside. The merman rowed them through the treacherous black rocks. Princess Aurantica sat stiff and straight. Phoenix sat facing her, and though it was hard to be certain in the dim light from the horn, it seemed to Phoenix that the princess was staring at her.

"Your Highness?" Phoenix asked. "Is something wrong?"

Princess Aurantica only shifted her gaze and looked out over the side of the gondola.

At last the black rocks ended, and they entered the open sea. The wall of mist loomed ahead, but now they glided under the stars, which seemed like chips of ice. Occasionally a breeze struck like a slap.

"Stop the gondola," Princess Aurantica commanded the merman. She stood up, swaying a little as the gondola rocked. The light from the sea dragon's horn cast a sickly yellow glow across her face. She reached into her skirt pocket and drew out a silver dagger in a sheath. With a sweep of her arm, she pulled the dagger from the sheath, then cast the sheath into the sea. She looked down at Phoenix.

"I am sorry, but I cannot allow you to reveal our secret and keep my sisters and me from our one pleasure in this life. The binding spell on your tongue may fail." She held up the dagger; a diamond glittered in the hilt, cold, hard, white.

26

The Third Night

PHOENIX, GRIPPING THE SIDES OF THE gondola with both hands, stared up at Princess Aurantica holding the silver dagger. The stars in the black sky encircled the princess's head like a crown.

"You're going to kill me?" Phoenix asked. Her eyes darted from left to right, seeking a way to escape. She could jump overboard. But she was too far out at sea; she would drown before reaching the shore. She could fight. But Princess Aurantica was a foot taller, and she had the dagger and the merman, too. Phoenix could see no hint of mercy in her face, only intense determination.

"Understand," Princess Aurantica said, "I have no wish to do this foul deed. But you have left me no choice. You should never have interfered. My sisters and I must dance before the black dragon's flame. Nothing else matters."

"I swear I won't reveal your secret," Phoenix said. Sweat was pooling between her shoulder blades. Her tongue seemed too large for her mouth. "I swear on Nemaree, the Sea Maid, and Kloud."

The princess shook her head. "I don't need to take the risk of trusting you."

Need. Phoenix dug her nails into her palms. That was the answer. She had to give the princess a reason to need her.

"It would be a mistake to kill me," she said.

"Why?"

"Because I can help you and your sisters."

"Help us?" The princess raised her eyebrows. "Doubtful. How?"

"I could . . ." Phoenix thought fast. What could she do? What? What? She stared at the dagger in the princess's hand. Her gaze slid down to the princess's thin white wrist, then to the cuff on her silver dress, the cuff that reached almost to her elbow, the cuff with the long row of tiny pearl buttons with two in the middle *undone*.

"Why, I could help you dress!" Phoenix exclaimed. "When you were in the wardrobe chamber putting on your dresses, I noticed that all of you have trouble fastening your buttons and laces, and tying your bows. You're not used to dressing yourselves without your ladies-in-waiting. Look at those two buttons undone on your cuff there. If I helped you dress, you could finish faster and get to the dancing much sooner."

Princess Aurantica examined her cuff. "How slovenly,"

she said. "I suppose a maid in the wardrobe chamber might be helpful." But she did not sound convinced.

Phoenix clasped her hands together. What else? What else did she have to offer the princesses? She imagined the dagger slicing across her throat, the hot blood trickling down her skin onto her red dress, her body tossed into the sea for the fish to eat.

"It is not enough," Princess Aurantica said. "I am sorry." She took a step forward, and for a moment, her dress swung backward and the toe of her white slipper was exposed, a beacon, a salvation.

"Wait!" Phoenix cried. "I know. I could be your own private shoemaker. For all twelve of you."

The princess stopped, her head tipped, considering. "Now that . . ." she said at last, "that would be worth keeping you alive." She lowered the dagger.

Phoenix let out a deep breath.

"But you would have to spend your life in the wardrobe room," the princess said. "You could never return to the world. We would bring you food each night, and all the tools and materials you would need to make our shoes. And you would help us dress. Do you agree to this?"

Phoenix nodded, willing to agree to anything to survive.

"Very well," Princess Aurantica said. She tossed the dagger into the sea. "Proceed," she ordered the merman. The gondola slipped forward again.

Phoenix leaned back, closed her eyes, and sighed. Her arms and legs felt weak and watery. Soon the silvery mist enveloped them, and the song of the flame began. Then they reached the ship.

Once onboard, Princess Aurantica rushed to the bow and immediately began dancing with her merman. The other princesses were already there. The red light from the black dragon's flame flickered on their throats and faces. The masked wizard danced with each of them, his black cloak swirling, just as he had the night before. The wild singing voice of the flame soared up and plummeted down. Phoenix could not hold herself back. As she threw her arms over her head, she smiled and laughed with delight. She spun on one foot, then the other. The flame grew brighter and brighter until, as before, it seemed to burn inside her.

Then Princess Osea collapsed. She lay on the deck, her eyes closed, her chest rising and falling faintly. The others merely danced around her. For a moment, for a heartbeat only, Phoenix hesitated, but when the masked wizard threw back his head and laughed, she laughed, too, and began to dance again. As she did, she forgot everything. Only the flame and the song and the dancing mattered—the curving sweep of her arm, the pounding stamp of her feet, the high note that sent her leaping through the air so that for a moment she was a bird, flying, suspended, existing only on the song until she came down and touched the deck again.

Another princess fell, and another. Each time the masked wizard laughed. Each time Phoenix, the mermen, and the other princesses kept dancing.

Then, out of nowhere, Whelk sprang onto the deck.

Whelk? What was he doing here, Phoenix wondered.

"Stop this, you fiend!" the boy shouted, throwing down the magic cloak. "You're killing these girls!"

The masked wizard spun on one foot and turned toward him. Sizing up his challenger, he laughed again. "Yes, and when they are all dead my revenge upon the queen will be complete." As he spoke the music grew quieter.

Still dancing, though not so wildly as before, Phoenix felt her mind beginning to clear. Whether this was because the masked wizard had focused his attention on Whelk or because she was jolted by Whelk's sudden appearance she did not know.

The remaining princesses kept dancing, but soon another princess fell and then another. Each time, the flame roaring from the black dragon's mouth surged higher. As Phoenix's mind cleared, she remember her plan to put out the flame, break the spell, and save the princesses. She guessed that Whelk had risked his life to come and distract the wizard while she extinguished the flame. But she loved the flame, loved it, adored it.

And what of touching the black dragon's heart? What of the cure for her illness?

The masked wizard took three menacing steps toward Whelk.

"Where is the wizard who helped you break my spells and find your way through the mist to this ship? I will destroy him." He turned and shouted toward the stern. "Show yourself!"

"No one helped me," Whelk said, defiant.

The masked wizard's head went back. "Impossible. You cannot have such power. You're only a boy, a bumbling boy."

Princess Aurantica collapsed onto the deck. Jolted again, Phoenix stopped dancing and knelt beside her. "Get up, Princess Aurantica, please." But the princess did not move, though she still breathed. "Don't die, Aurantica," Phoenix cried, shaking her. "I can't let you die."

The masked wizard's back was turned toward Phoenix. She darted toward the bow and the black dragon. She climbed up onto the dragon's leg, then onto its wing. Her shoes kept slipping on the smooth black metal. The sea frothed beneath her as the ship rose and dipped. If she fell, no one would save her: she would drown.

"You talk of revenge upon the queen," Whelk said. "Why?"

"You of all people should know that," the masked wizard said. "Because she murdered your father, my dear brother, Kyriad."

"Uncle?" Whelk gasped. *Uncle?*

Phoenix glanced over her shoulder and saw the masked wizard rip off his dragon mask. She could not see his face but knew from Whelk's horrified expression that it must be Fengal.

"The queen could have been merciful," Fengal said, "but she hung Kyriad, the dearest thing to my heart. And now I will kill her daughters, the dearest things to her heart. I will let her suffer the pain of that, and then I will seize her throne and kill her, too."

"It can't be," Whelk said, his voice small and uncertain.

"And why not?"

"Because . . . because I could bear the shame about Father since I had you to look up to. A great, grand wizard fighting for good. You're a member of the High Council of Wizards. A leader of the Archipelago Party. An adviser to the queen."

"Mere ruses to confuse my enemies."

"But I've always wanted to be like you. And now you're, you're . . ."

"You can be like me," Fengal said. "Think, boy. After I take over the kingdom, you will be my heir. I'll teach you everything I know about wizardry, all the spells, all the words of power. Isn't that what you've always wanted?"

"Yes," Whelk said slowly. "It's what I've always wanted. Always."

Phoenix reached the black dragon's back and straddled it, gripping the sides with her knees. Arching, white-tipped spray brushed her legs. She inched upward. At last she reached the crystal window.

Beneath the crystal, wreathed in flame, the black dragon's heart pulsed. Phoenix reached under her petticoat and yanked the hammer off its string. She raised her arm high and brought the hammer down on the crystal window. There was no sound, no scratch, not even a dent. She hit again, harder. Again, there was no sound; the crystal seemed to absorb the blow, but this time a tiny crack had formed. Phoenix beat on the window again and again; a few more spindly cracks appeared.

She looked back over her shoulder. More princesses had fallen. By the time she broke the crystal window, they could all be dead, or Fengal could have caught her. She had to pour the sand down the black dragon's throat and break the spell before it was too late. She had to choose between a cure for her illness and the lives of the princesses.

"Why do you hesitate, boy?" Fengal said, his attention still fixed on Whelk. "Your choice is clear. Always choose power. So what if the princesses are dead? They are nothing compared with the glorious life you will live."

And Phoenix knew then that she could not live a glorious life, even if she were well, if the princesses were dead. And, her heart whispered, she could keep the Kingdom of Brilliance.

She dropped the hammer into the sea, grabbed the sand from under her petticoat, then shimmied up the black dragon's neck, which grew warmer the higher she went. Its head was bent back, and the flame roared and twisted like a living thing straight upward from its mouth. Her face glowed from the heat. She peered back at Whelk, standing undecided beside his uncle. Would Whelk join him? She had to hurry and dump in the sand before he did.

Fengal stretched out his hand. "You'll be the greatest wizard in the kingdom next to me. There's power in you, boy. I see that now. Power that you have not even imagined. And after I die you'll be king, ruler of all Windward."

Phoenix, riding the black dragon, had almost reached its mouth. She shimmied higher, stretched out one hand, put it down on the black dragon's head, and screamed. Pain seared through her as her hand burned on the hot metal. She snatched it away. Fengal spun around.

"Get away from the flame!" he shouted.

Phoenix shook her hand back and forth, blew on it, then cradled it with her other hand, crying and moaning.

Fengal raised his hand toward her, but Whelk leaped forward and struck it aside.

"Don't hurt her!" he exclaimed. "I want to be a wizard more than anything, but not at the price of the princesses' lives or Phoenix's. I don't want to be like you. I don't want anything to do with you."

"Stupid boy, you'll never be like me," Fengal said. "You'll be nothing but a lowly shoemaker all your life."

"I'm a shoemaker with some power, Uncle," Whelk said. And he held out his hand, said three words, and froze his uncle in place.

"Now, Phoenix, now!" Whelk cried. "The sand!"

But Phoenix was having trouble untying the knot with her burned hand. Pain shot up her arm. Sweat from the heat of the flame dripped down her forehead into her eyes, mixing with tears. At last the knot came free. She began lifting the bag to pour the sand into the black dragon's mouth, then stopped. The flame dancing before her eyes was so beautiful, so alive, with little curling edges of blue and gold. *Break the spell!* part of her whispered, *break the spell!* But the flame! The beautiful singing flame! She looked down at the deck, at the prostrate bodies of the princesses; all of them had fallen. "Aurantica, Osea, Batissa." She whispered their names. For them . . . she had to destroy the flame for them.

Then, as she was about to upend the bag of sand, a gust of wind pushed the edge of her red silk cloak into the flame. It caught fire. She dropped the bag of sand in her lap, ripped off her cloak, and threw it behind her. The wind caught the burning cloak and blew it up against one of the sails, the lower part just visible at the edge of the mist. The cloak hung, suspended, a burning blot against the purple sail. Then the fire leaped to the sail, and it burst into flame.

Fengal moved again. He laughed. "Yes, dear nephew, I see you have some power, but not enough." He raised one hand and sent Whelk flying through the air. The boy landed on his back on the deck ten feet away.

As Fengal whipped around toward Phoenix, she poured the sand into the dragon's mouth. Immediately, the flame, smothered, hissed and then died, leaving a long tail of greenish black smoke. The music stopped. The mermen disappeared.

Fengal screamed. He began to writhe and darken; then he dissolved into a column of greenish black smoke that curled away in the air. All that was left of him was the gold dragon ring lying on the deck; its ruby sparkled once and then turned black.

The silvery enchanted mist wreathing the ship vanished. But the ship and the sails were not enchanted. The three masts loomed up against the stars, their purple sails full of wind. The fire was not an enchantment either. Flames jumped from the blazing sail and raced up the rigging, setting ablaze first one sail, then another. And the twelve princesses lay scattered on the deck of the burning ship.

27

The Burning Ship

PHOENIX SCOOTED DOWN THE BLACK dragon and jumped back onto the deck as the flames roared and crackled overhead. She ran to Whelk. His eyes were closed.

"Whelk! Whelk!" She shook him. "Wake up. The ship is on fire!"

He opened his eyes, groaned, and touched the back of his head.

"Where's my uncle?" he asked, sitting up.

"Gone. Dead or something. Vanished anyway. The flame's out. The spell's broken. But the ship's on fire. We have to get off, get the princesses off. Can you stand?"

Whelk got to his hands and knees, then stood. When he bent back his head and looked up at the burning sails, his eyes widened.

"In Nemaree's Name." Then he looked out. "We're not so far away from land after all. Just beyond the mouth of the bay. The enchanted mist kept us from seeing out as well as people from seeing the ship."

"And the ship isn't being steered by magic anymore either." Phoenix pointed. "Look. We're headed straight for the rocks on Shipwreck Point."

She ran over and tried to wake Princess Aurantica. The crown of seaweed, kelp, and barnacles her merman had given her had fallen from her head.

"Aurantica!" she cried. "You must wake up. The ship is on fire and headed for the rocks." But, though Phoenix shook her and patted her cheeks, the princess did not stir. "What are we going to do?" Phoenix cried.

"I expect the gondolas have vanished, too. Go see. If they have, try to lower the lifeboat," Whelk said. "We'll have to get them into it somehow."

"Can you use magic to transport them to the lifeboat?"

"I don't know. Go. I'll try to figure something out."

Phoenix ran along the deck and peered down the rope ladder. The gondolas had vanished. She raced to the lifeboat. Fortunately, it was on a winch, and she had no problem launching it by herself in spite of her burned hand. It splashed down into the water and bobbed beside the ship, attached with ropes. Another rope ladder led to it. But how would they get the princesses down the ladder?

She looked up. Tongues of fire frolicked among the sails, skipping and leaping, running up and down, back and forth. Entire sheets burned. A blazing timber dropped onto the deck, and sparks flew in every direction. She kicked it overboard. Soon the deck would be littered with burning debris falling from above. Then the deck itself would catch fire.

Whelk came up. He had his arms under Princess Aurantica's shoulders and was dragging her along the deck.

"I thought if I could at least get her closer to the lifeboat . . ." he said, panting.

"But we can't possibly carry the princesses down the rope ladder," Phoenix said. "You have to wake them up."

"I tried. I can't. I don't know enough magic."

"Try again."

"It's no use." Whelk laid Princess Aurantica down and straightened. "We have to save ourselves."

"And leave the princesses to die?"

"There's nothing else to do." Whelk swung one leg over the deck onto the rope ladder. "Come on."

"You can't just leave them! If you do, you're as bad as your father and uncle."

"What do you know about it!" Whelk shouted. He swung his leg back onto the deck and stood glaring at her.

Phoenix glared back. "I know that what Fengal said about you is true. That you have power you haven't even dreamed of. You have to find it. Now!"

"You don't understand. I'm nothing but a shoemaker. A stupid, lowly shoemaker who knows a handful of magic spells and—" Suddenly, a faraway look came into Whelk's eyes, and he tipped his head to one side. "A shoemaker who knows a handful of magic spells," he repeated softly. "That's it!" he exclaimed.

"What?" Phoenix asked.

But Whelk knelt at Princess Aurantica's feet, held up his hands, and began to speak. *"Et illachus bonea e tacatta shoemakium—sprago!"*

A swirl of green light spiraled around Princess Aurantica's feet, exploding with tiny silver stars and sparkling rose red fountains. Gradually the light settled into a pair of shining shoes upon her feet.

"Oh!" Phoenix exclaimed.

"Walk to me," Whelk commanded, pointing at the shoes. Though her eyes were still closed, Princess Aurantica drew herself to a sitting position, slowly stood, walked up to Whelk, and stopped.

"Climb down the ladder into the boat." Whelk pointed at the shoes again.

The princess, or the shoes, did as he said.

Phoenix peered over the railing, watching the princess settle down in the lifeboat. "It works!"

"Come on," Whelk said. "Let's do the same thing with the others."

They ran back to the bow, where the other princesses still lay on the deck. One by one, as Whelk made them magic shoes, Phoenix led the princesses to the ladder, dodging the burning timbers that rained down from above. When there were two princesses left, the deck began to burn. The heat grew intense as the flames roared. Sweat dripped down Phoenix's face and back.

"Hurry, Whelk!" she cried. When the last princess was in the boat, Whelk and Phoenix scurried down the ladder. Whelk cut the ropes with his pocketknife. He took one oar and Phoenix took the other, but the lifeboat barely moved. The boat, not meant for fourteen people, even if twelve of them were thin as wraiths, rode dangerously low in the water.

"I'll swim," Phoenix said.

"You'll drown," Whelk said.

"I'll hang on to the rope and kick. When I get tired, I'll let you pull me. Come on, we've got to get away from the ship." She took off her shoes and slipped into the cold water. After Whelk threw her the rope, he began to row. The lifeboat started to move. She swam, kicking her legs, clutching the rope, which chafed her burned hand. When they had gone a good distance, she stopped swimming, let the rope take her weight, and looked back over her shoulder. She gasped.

The ship looked like a roaring inferno against the black night. The sails were long gone, but the masts, the deck, and the hull blazed red and orange and gold, with flames writhing like snakes. The water around the ship glistened with reflected light. Plumes of fire shot out the portholes. Flames roared around the black dragon on the prow. Even as she watched, the ship rammed into the rocks on Shipwreck Point. The hull caved in. A mast toppled, crashing through the deck and tipping the whole ship starboard until it slowly sank beneath the sea.

Phoenix started to swim again. Her body was shaking now, and she was too cold. She peered ahead through the darkness to measure how far away the shore was, but she could see nothing. Her legs grew leaden. She held on to the rope and let Whelk pull her through the water. She could not last much longer. Then, just when she thought she would surely drown, she saw another boat, a lantern shining in the bow, coming toward them.

"Help!" she cried. "We need help. We have the princesses!"

28

True Brilliance

SILENCE!" QUEEN ZANDORA SAID TO Phoenix the next morning as she and Whelk stood before her in the palace drawing room. Sunlight poured through the tall windows and splashed over the queen's red velvet shoes, making the rhinestone-studded buckles sparkle.

Last night, after the boat had rescued them, the princesses had been taken back to the palace. Now they were all resting safely in their beds, attended by Mederi Gale. With time and care and rest, the mederi had said, they all would recover.

"But, Your Majesty," Phoenix said, waving her bandaged hands. "I—"

"I said, silence!" the queen exclaimed. "I have never heard anyone talk as much as you, child."

Phoenix, who felt the bees buzzing inside her, had been

talking and talking about everything that had happened—Fengal's plot, the black dragon's flame, the wild dancing, how she and Whelk had broken the spell, the burning ship—repeating herself in zigs and zags. The binding spell on her tongue had ended when Fengal vanished. But she knew her babbling came because she had been taking only a quarter of her potion. She kept shifting her weight from one leg to the other. The urge to talk was like a wave inside her.

"Now, if I can get a word in edgewise," the queen said. "Whelk, you said that Fengal told you his position as an adviser to me was a mere ruse?"

"Yes, Your Majesty."

She shook her head, and the crystal beads sewn around the white bodice of her dress tinkled. "How could I have been so blind?" she asked. "Fengal acted as the head of the Archipelago Party to spy on them for me. Slowly I began to trust him, and he entered my inner circle of advisers who plan each step in our war with the Order of the Black Dragon. And then the villain used his position to spy on me for them." She twisted a gold ring on her finger. "No wonder the war has not been going well. Evil man! Were he not dead I would hang him and bury him in the ground instead of in the sanctified sea. Both for his treason and for what he did to my daughters.

"But now," she said, smiling, "let us turn our attention to those who have nobly served the realm. In the proclamation I sent out, I declared that whoever saved the princesses would receive the hand of the youngest princess in marriage as well as the Duchy of the Islands of Trebonness in the Western Reach. The princesses' secret would not have been discovered without your help."

"I—" Phoenix began.

The queen held up one hand. "However, I am rescinding the offer of my daughter's hand in marriage. The princesses have explained that they believe they fell under Fengal's spell because I arranged their marriages without their consent. They have, in fact, absolutely refused to go through with them." The queen paused, a look of amazement on her face behind her silver spectacles. "Absolutely refused. In light of all the circumstances, I have decided to abide by their wishes. All that matters to me is that my dear daughters be well and happy again." She pressed a lace-edged handkerchief to her lips.

"What about Trebonness?" Phoenix squeaked out. Then she put one hand over her mouth.

"The offer of the duchy still stands," said the queen. "So here we have a problem. There are two of you. I cannot give you both the duchy."

"If it please Your Majesty," Whelk said, "there is something else I'd rather have."

"And what is that?" asked the queen.

"I'd like to go to the wizards' school on Honorath. I've been saving up for the passage."

"Done," said the queen. "And you may keep your savings. Therefore, Phoenix Dance, I am giving you the duchy. I will have the papers drawn up immediately." She paused. "And as I recall, Phoenix, when you first came to me you wanted your appointment as Shoemaker to the Royal Household restored. Do you still wish that?"

"Oh, yes, Your Majesty," Phoenix said. "Yes, yes." She pressed her hand against her stomach to keep the words rushing inside her from spilling out.

"It is restored, Your Grace," said the queen.

"Your Grace?" asked Phoenix.

"That is your new title. You are now a duchess."

"Oh, but it's my aunts who should be the duchesses, not me."

"No indeed. You helped discover the secret," the queen said, "so the title is yours."

The bees were still buzzing inside Phoenix later that night as she celebrated at home with her aunts. Her aunts were ecstatic about Trebonness—well, two of them anyway.

"To think you won Trebonness back," said Aunt Liona, waltzing Phoenix around the parlor. "That's spectacular, Duchess Dance!"

"I'm so proud of you for saving the princesses," said Aunt Twisle. "For putting their safety before your own. Trebonness was a fitting reward."

"We truly have Trebonness back?" Aunt Mulgaussy asked. "I never dreamed . . . not really." She grabbed a hat with a purple feather off the costume rack and fanned herself. "Not really. No, I must say I never thought we'd really . . . What shall we do? We have our lives here."

"What do you mean, what shall we do?" cried Aunt Liona. "We've heard nothing but Trebonness this and Trebonness that from you for years. And now you're asking what we should do? Why, go there, of course!"

"But I can't leave." Phoenix sat down on the sofa. "I'm Shoemaker to the Royal Household! I have responsibilities. The princesses won't be wearing their shoes out like before, now that the enchantment is broken, but there are still lots of shoes to make. Lots and lots and lots! Surely Percy Snailkips will let me keep my job now that I have the royal appointment back. He has to. He just has to!"

Aunt Liona sat down beside her and poked her arm. "I tell you what we'll do. Mulgaussy and Twisle will go to Trebonness and manage things there. I'll stay here with the Seven Sea Stars and you for as long as you want to be Shoemaker to the Royal Household. We can go for visits to Trebonness—it's only five days' journey by ship from Faranor. Will that suit everyone?"

They all agreed. But Phoenix, her mind skipping and racing, was thinking about something else.

"What's the matter, Phoenix?" Aunt Liona asked. "You look puzzled."

"It's that evil old Fengal." She drummed her fingers on the table. "He said, more or less, that he would have killed me—"

"Killed you!" all three aunts exclaimed.

Phoenix nodded. "Killed me. Except that I looked like someone who had once been dear to him. And guess what? It was Mother."

"Oh, of course. I'd almost forgotten," Aunt Twisle said. "Fengal tried to court her once, before she met your father, but she would have nothing to do with him."

"Then she was smart," said Phoenix. She thought about her failed courtship with Whelk. It had been so hard to say goodbye to him on the palace steps and watch him walk away, limping slightly, to disappear into magic lands.

There was a knock on the door. Phoenix jumped up and answered it.

"A letter for Phoenix Dance," a messenger said, holding out a folded piece of paper.

"Who's it from?" asked Aunt Twisle when Phoenix had shut the door.

"Rora." Phoenix popped the brown sealing wax, unfolded the note, and read Rora's tiny, slanting script.

Dear Phoenix,
I have been stricken *to the soul. To the very soul! That Fengal—he that I thought the mightiest champion of the Archipelago Party—should instead be its greatest TRAITOR! Spying on us for the queen. There can be no greater calumny. Vile! Base! Foul! Since that moment I learned his true nature I have suffered the severest TORMENT.*

And you, Phoenix Dance, killed the fiend. I am so

proud of you! At last you have proven *your loyalty to the party. In light of these events, I am writing to say that I have decided to* forgive *you, mostly, for abandoning me that night in Parliament Square. You must never, never forget that you wronged me TERRIBLY then, but I will now permit you to be my friend once more.*

RORA

P.S. You might have let the foul fiend finish off the princesses *before you killed him. But I shall overlook it.* This *time.*

Phoenix shook her head. She could not quite smile, though, because she was not quite sure that she had forgiven Rora. But probably, in time, she would.

That night, though Phoenix was exhausted, she could not sleep. She bunched her pillow, wadded her quilt, moved her legs into a crouch, stretched them back out, and then turned on her other side and did it all over again. The pain in her chest was growing worse. The bees inside her hummed louder and louder. Three hours later, when the tower clock was striking two, she was still awake.

"I'm tired!" she whispered, almost crying with frustration. "I'm so tired." Her thoughts spun in her head. Again and again she saw the flame shooting from the black dragon's mouth, the beautiful flame. Again and again she saw the burning ship, utterly destroyed because she had set it on fire.

Phoenix squeezed her eyes shut. She knew she had passed

the threshold of the Kingdom of Brilliance and was heading for its frenzied heart.

"No," she whispered. "I want to stay on the threshold. Stay on the edge! I can do it, I can. I'm strong enough!" But she was not strong enough. She slapped her pillow. She could not control the Kingdom of Brilliance. It compelled her, possessed her, obliterating all her choices about what to do and who to be.

Each time she became filled with the power of delighted brilliance, with fire—which deep down she knew was really sickness—Phoenix saw she would have to find the strength to put out the fire before she destroyed herself. Because of her illness, she would have to face that moment again and again throughout her life. She thought of the black dragon ship, then of the ship *Phoenix Dance* from her dreams. Not once but a hundred times, a thousand times, the *Phoenix Dance* with burning sails would speed across the water. Where would she find the strength to put out the flame? To pull herself away from the perilous lure of the Kingdom of Brilliance? She thought about the destruction the Kingdom of Brilliance had caused in her life: she had lost Whelk because of it, she might lose her job because of it, she had lost hours of her life in the Kingdom of Darkness because of it, she had almost let the princesses die because of it.

She got up and walked into the kitchen. She looked at the covered slop pail, where her discarded potion lay amid the dinner scraps—the turnip peelings, bean shells, and tea leaves. Phoenix laid a fire in the stove and lit it. The flames curled up, reflecting off the black walls. When the fire was snapping, she put the teakettle on to boil.

She remembered something Queen Zandora had said. *How simple a thing, to be well. We do not appreciate how sacred a thing it is when we have it. Only when it is gone do we realize how powerful a thing it is, simply to be well.*

Phoenix took down a brown earthenware canister from the shelf, opened it, and stared at the herbs that formed the base for her potion. She hated the smell of them; they smelled of dullness, fatness, pimples, and nausea. She hated the look of them, the brown leaves, the purple flowers, the yellow stems.

I've been fighting the wrong way, she heard Rora say.

Phoenix closed her eyes. Had she been fighting the wrong way, too? Again she pictured the *Phoenix Dance* with the burning sails. What did the ship look like without the burning sails? What color were the sails? Who was she without the illness? She remembered what Mederi Gale had said, "I'm certain your real voice is in there somewhere, waiting for you to be well long enough so it can come out."

She curled her bandaged hand into a fist and winced. She had put out the fire that dazzled the princesses. Could she put out the fire that dazzled her? The fire of the Kingdom of Brilliance?

Phoenix measured two teaspoons of the herbs from the canister into the tea strainer; she had watched her aunts do this many times, though she had never done it herself.

When she dropped the strainer into a yellow ceramic cup that had a nick in the rim, it clinked in the bottom. As soon as the teakettle began to boil, Phoenix picked it up and poured the hot water over the tea strainer, filling the cup. The rising steam dampened her face. She breathed in the steam and felt it shoot like a wet beam down her throat. When the cup was full, she covered it with a saucer to steep for five minutes.

Phoenix tapped the hot cup with her fingertips. She did not want it; she did want it; that contradiction would always be true. But in the cup was the only true power she had to fight her illness. The power to take the potion, the power to be well. She could choose to be well. She could choose to have the ship of herself sail on more tranquil seas—without burning sails—sail to far, beautiful places without crashing upon rocks. She could choose to leave the brilliance and the fire behind.

But the same wind that filled the sails on the ship spoke to her of another kind of brilliance—true brilliance, true power. The brilliance of sleeping every night and waking refreshed every morning. The brilliance of talking so that people could understand her, instead of in a rushing stream. The brilliance of steadily doing work she loved every day. The brilliance of being well.

Phoenix removed the saucer and strainer and picked up the cup. She glanced at the slop pail. It was not too late; she could still throw the potion out. If she did, though, she might never find out who she really was, might never discover the color of her sails.

The heat of the potion flowed through the sides of the cup and warmed her hand. "Put out the fire," she whispered. The bitter steam curled into her nose as Phoenix raised the cup to her lips, tipped back her head, and drank.

Author's Note

Phoenix's illness, called in her world the Illness of the Two Kingdoms, is based on a real illness in our world called bipolar disorder or manic-depressive illness. This illness causes dramatic swings in a person's mood. These swings in mood range from feelings of being overly "high," excited, and/or irritable to feelings of being terribly sad and hopeless. The high feelings are called mania (in Phoenix's world, the Kingdom of Brilliance). The low feelings are called depression (in Phoenix's world, the Kingdom of Darkness). These mood swings are severe, different from the normal ups and downs that everyone experiences. They don't happen only once, but over and over again, back and forth like a pendulum. Sometimes people feel normal for a while, but sooner or later they become depressed or manic again.

This illness affects both adults and children, men and women, roughly 1.5 percent of the population. There is no single cause for bipolar disorder—rather, many things act together to produce it. But it is partly caused by a biochemical imbalance in the brain. Bipolar disorder is also passed genetically—it runs in certain families who are prone to this illness.

The most severe type of the illness is called Bipolar I Disorder. Bipolar II Disorder is a milder form where a person has a less intense form of mania called hypomania. Phoenix has Bipolar II Disorder. At first hypomania may feel wonderful. Sometimes the person who has it becomes highly productive and creative and may deny that anything is wrong, as Phoenix does. But without treatment the person can become sicker and sicker and may even swing into depression, again as Phoenix does.

Like diabetes or heart disease, bipolar disorder is a long-term illness that must be carefully managed throughout a person's life. There is no cure. Since the twentieth century, however, medications called mood stabilizers have been available to treat this illness. So now many people who have bipolar disorder can lead normal lives. But they must take their medications all the time, even when they feel well, because the medications help prevent the mood swings and keep them from being as severe. Sometimes people have a hard time staying on their medications. This is because, as Phoenix discovers, they can have unpleasant side effects and make a person feel that life seems different from before. But taking medication is the only hope people with bipolar disorder have to lead normal lives.

More people all the time are being diagnosed with bipolar disorder. Like Phoenix, I also have Bipolar II Disorder. I have wanted to write a book about it for a long time, but I was waiting for the right idea. Then one day I reread Grimm's fairy tale of the Twelve Dancing Princesses, which I had always loved as a child. It immediately caught my attention. Surely princesses who danced so hard each night that they wore out their shoes were in a manic state, just like people who have bipolar disorder?

My imagination began to work and I thought of many questions that the fairy tale did not answer. For example, what would the princesses be like in the daytime after all their manic dancing at night? Wouldn't they be terribly tired and depressed? Wouldn't they grow more exhausted each day until they were as worn out as the worn-out shoes? It seemed to me that the princesses had a rapidly cycling form of bipolar disorder—but their illness was caused by a magic spell cast upon them. I thought it would be interesting to retell the fairy tale with this in mind.

But the story needed a heart. That is why I chose to center it on one ordinary girl whose bipolar disorder was real, not caused by a spell. That's where Phoenix comes in—as the shoemaker for the princesses. I wrote this book because I want young people to experience the story of one particular girl with bipolar disorder and the challenges she faces. But Phoenix's story is only one story. Each person with bipolar disorder has a different story to tell.